THE SPRAYING STREAM SEPARATED THE CAT AND TURKEY.

The Bobbsey Twins at Meadow Brook *Frontispiece (Page 112)*

The Bobbsey Twins at Meadow Brook

BY

LAURA LEE HOPE

AUTHOR OF "THE BOBBSEY TWINS," "THE BOBBSEY TWINS AT SNOW LODGE," "THE BOBBSEY TWINS ON A HOUSEBOAT," .

NEW YORK
GROSSET & DUNLAP
PUBLISHERS

Made in the United States of America

The Bobbsey Twins at Meadow Brook

CONTENTS

THE BOBBSEY TWINS AT MEADOW BROOK

CHAPTER I

A CROCKERY CRASH

"WELL, here we are back home again!" exclaimed Nan Bobbsey, as she sat down in a chair on the porch. "Oh, but we have had *such* a good time!"

"The best ever!" exclaimed her brother Bert, as he set down the valise he had been carrying, and walked back to the front gate to take a small satchel from his mother.

"I'm going to carry mine! I want to carry mine all the way!" cried little fat Freddie Bobbsey, thinking perhaps his bigger brother might want to take, too, his bundle.

"All right, you can carry your own, Freddie," said Bert, pleasantly. "But it's pretty heavy for you."

"It—it isn't very heavy," panted Freddie,

as he struggled on with his bundle, his short fat legs fairly "twinkling" to and fro as he came up the walk. "It's got some cookies in, too, my bundle has; and Flossie and I are going to eat 'em when we get on the porch."

"Oh, so that's the reason you didn't want Bert to take your package, is it?" asked Mrs. Bobbsey, with a smile, as she patted the little fat chap on the head.

"Oh, well, I'll give Bert a cookie if he wants one," said Freddie, generously, "but I'm strong enough to carry my own bundle all the way; aren't I, Dinah?" and he appealed to a fat, good-natured looking colored woman, who was waddling along, carrying a number of packages.

"Dat's what yo' is, honey lamb! Dat's what yo' is!" Dinah exclaimed. "An' ef I could see dat man ob mine, Sam Johnson, I'd make him take some ob dese yeah t'ings."

As Dinah spoke there came from around the corner of the house a tall, slim colored man, who as soon as he saw the party of returning travelers, ran forward to help them carry their luggage

"Well, it's about time dat yo' come t' help us, Sam Johnson!" exclaimed his wife. "It's about time!"

"Didn't know yo' all was a-comin', Dinah! Didn't know yo' all would get heah so soon, 'deed I didn't!" Sam exclaimed, with a laugh, that showed his white teeth in strange contrast to his black face. "Freddie, shall I take yo' package? Flossie, let me reliebe yo', little Missie!"

"No, Sam, thank you!" answered the little girl, who was just about the size and build of Freddie. "I have only Snoop, our cat, and I can carry him easily enough. You help Dinah!"

"'Deed an' he had better help me!" exclaimed the colored cook.

Sam took all the packages he could carry, and hurried with them to the stoop. But he had not gone very far before something happened.

From behind him rushed a big dog, barking and leaping about, glad, probably, to be home again from part of the summer vacation.

"Look out, Sam!" called Bert Bobbsey,

who was carrying the valise his mother had had. "Look out!"

"What's de mattah? Am I droppin' suffin?" asked Sam, trying to turn about and look at all the bundles and packages he had in his arms and hands.

"It's Snap!" cried Nan, who was sitting comfortably on the shady porch. "Look out for him, Sam."

"Snap! Behave yourself!" ordered little fat Flossie, as she set down a wooden cage containing a black cat. "Be good, Snap!"

"Here, Snap! Snap! Come here!" called Freddie.

Snap, the big dog, was too excited just then to mind. With another loud, joyous bark he rushed up behind Sam, and, as the colored man of all work about the Bobbsey place had very bow, or curved, legs, Snap ran right between them. That is, he ran half way, and then, as he was a pretty fat dog, he stuck there.

"Good land ob massy!" exclaimed Sam, as he looked down to see the dog half way between his bow legs, Snap's head sticking out one way, and his wagging tail the other. "Get out ob dat, Snap!" cried Sam. "Get out! Move on, sah!"

"Bow wow!" barked Snap, which might have meant almost anything.

"Look out!" shouted Sam. "Yo'll upset me! Dat's what you will!"

And indeed it did seem as though this might happen. For Sam was so laden down with packages that he could not balance himself very well, and had almost toppled over.

"Here, Snap!" called Bert, who was laughing so hard that he could hardly stand up, for really it was a funny sight.

"Don't call him, Bert," advised Mrs. Bobbsey. "If you do he'll run out, and then Sam surely will be knocked over. And there are some fresh eggs in one of those packages he took from Dinah."

Snap himself did not seem to know what to do. There he was, tightly held fast, his fat sides between Sam's bow legs. Snap could go neither forward nor backward just then. He barked and wagged his tail, for he knew it was all in fun.

"Open your legs wider, Sam, man!" exclaimed his wife. "Den de dorg kin git out!"

Sam, holding tightly to the packages, did manage to stoop down and so spread his legs a little farther apart. This released Snap, who, with a happy bark, and a wild wagging of his tail, bounded up on the stoop where Nan sat.

A little later the whole Bobbsey family, with the exception of Mr. Bobbsey, were sitting comfortably in the porch chairs, while Sam was opening the front shutters, having already unlocked the front door for the returning family.

"Home again!" exclaimed Mrs. Bobbsey, with a little sigh, as she looked around at the familiar scenes. "My, but how dusty it is after being on the lovely water."

"Yes'm, dey shuah has been lots ob dust!" exclaimed Sam. "We need rain mighty bad, an' I've had de garden hose goin' ebery night, too."

"I'll soon sweep off dish yeah porch," said Dinah. "Sam, yo' git me a broom."

"Oh, don't bother now, Dinah," said Mrs. Bobbsey. "Make a cup of tea, first. The dust doesn't matter, and we'll not be here long."

"Won't we?" exclaimed Nan. "Oh, where are we going next?"

"We'll talk about it as soon as your father comes home," said Mrs. Bobbsey, for her husband had stopped on the way from the houseboat dock, where the family had lately landed, to go to his lumber office for a little while.

"Let Snoop out!" begged little Flossie. "Snoop's tired of being shut up in that box." In order to carry him from the boat to the house Snoop had been put in a small traveling crate.

"I'll let him out as soon as I get a screwdriver," promised Bert. "My, but it's hot here!"

"Indeed it is," agreed his mother, who was fanning herself with her pocket handkerchief as she sat in a rocking-chair. "It isn't much like our nice houseboat, is it?"

"No, indeed," agreed Nan. "I wish we hadn't come home."

"And summer is only half over," went on Bert. "Here it is only August."

"Oh, well, there are plenty of good times ahead of you children yet, before school begins," said Mrs. Bobbsey. "Now let's see. Have we everything?" and she looked at the pile of bundles and valises on the porch.

"I guess we didn't forget anything, except papa," said Freddie. "And he's coming," he added, as the others laughed.

"Sam, am de fire made?" demanded Dinah. "I wants t' make a cup ob tea."

"Fire all made," reported the colored man. "I'll go git a fresh pail ob water now. I didn't know jest prezackly when yo' was comin'," he said to Mrs. Bobbsey, "or I'd a' been down to de dock t' meet de houseboat."

"Might a' come anyhow," muttered Dinah. "Yo' all didn't hab nuffin' t' do heah!"

"Huh! I didn't, eh?" cried Sam. "Nuffin t' do! Why, I cut de grass, an' fed de chickens, an' watered de lawn, an'—an'——"

"Go 'long wif yo'," ordered his wife with a laugh. "Bring in some mo' wood for de fire!"

"And get a screw-driver so I can let Snoop out," begged Flossie. "He's tired of being shut up in the crate!"

"Right away, Missie! Right away!" promised good-natured Sam.

A little later Snoop, the black cat, was stretching himself on the porch, while Snap, the big dog, rushed up and down the lawn, barking loudly to let all the neighbors' dogs know he was back home again—at least for a time.

Meanwhile Bert, as the "little man of the house," had brought in the packages and satchels from the porch. Nan was helping her mother get out a cool kimona, while Dinah was down in the kitchen getting ready a cup of tea for Mrs. Bobbsey.

Flossie and Freddie, as the youngest Bobbsey twins, had nothing in particular to do, so they ran about, here, there, everywhere, renewing acquaintance with the familiar objects about the yard—things they had forgotten during the two months they had been away on a houseboat, for part of their summer vacation.

"Oh, look! My flower-bed is full of weeds!" cried Flossie, as she came to a corner of the yard where she had set out some pansy plants just before going away.

"And I can't even see the lettuce I planted,"

said Freddie. "I guess Sam didn't weed our gardens."

"Never mind, we can make new ones," Flossie said. "Oh, Freddie, look! There's a strange cat!" Both children ran to where Snoop was making the acquaintance of a pussy friend. The cats seemed to like one another and the strange one let the little twins pet it as it lapped some milk from Snoop's saucer.

A little later Dinah called Flossie and Freddie into the house to have a glass of milk and some bread and jam, for it was past lunch time The small twins came willingly enough.

"What are we going to do the rest of the summer?" asked Nan, as she sat next to her mother at the table. "Are we going away again?"

"I hope so!" exclaimed Bert. "The houseboat suited me, but if we can have a trip to the seashore, or go to the country, so much the better."

"We shall see," half-promised Mrs. Bobbsey. "As soon as papa comes home from the office, he will know how much more time he can spare from business to go with us. Then I can tell you——"

"There he comes now, mamma!" exclaimed Nan. "Oh, excuse me for interrupting you," she went on, for Mrs. Bobbsey insisted upon the children being just as polite at home, and to one another, as they would be among strangers.

"That's all right, Nan," said her mother kindly. "When papa comes in, and has had a cup of tea, we'll talk over matters, and decide what to do."

"Well, are you all settled?" asked Mr. Bobbsey, as he came in, catching little Freddie up in his strong arms. "Haven't put out any fires since you got here, have you?" he asked, for Freddie had a great love for playing fireman, and he often put out "make-believe" blazes with a toy fire engine he had, which squirted real water.

"No alarms to-day," laughed Freddie, for his father was tickling him in his "fat ribs," as Freddie called them.

"How's my little fat fairy?" went on Mr.

Bobbsey, catching Flossie up as he had Freddie.

"All right," she answered. "Oh, papa, your whiskers prick!" she cried, as Mr. Bobbsey kissed her.

"Sit down and have a cup of tea," invited Mrs. Bobbsey. "Then we can talk about what we are to do. The children are anxious to get away again, and if we *are* to go there is no need of unpacking more than we have to."

"Would you like to go to Meadow Brook?" asked Mr. Bobbsey, looking at his happy family.

"You know I would," answered his wife, with a smile.

"Meadow Brook! Oh, are we going there?" cried Nan.

"Well, Uncle Daniel has sent us an invitation," said Mr. Bobbsey, "and your mother and I are thinking of it."

"Can you leave your lumber business long enough to go with us?" asked Mrs. Bobbsey.

"I think so," replied her husband. "I just stopped at the office, and everything there is going along nicely. So I think we'll go to

Meadow Brook, in the country, for the rest of the summer."

"Hurray! Hurrah! Oh, how nice!" cried the children.

"Dinah, I think I'll have another cup of tea," went on Mr. Bobbsey, as the colored cook waddled in. "Make it cold, this time--with ice in it. I am very warm."

"Yais-sah," said Dinah, taking his cup.

Then followed a confusion of talk, the two sets of twins doing the most. They were joyfully excited at the idea of going to Meadow Brook farm.

"I'm going to turn somersaults in the grass—just like this," cried Freddie, rolling over and over on the floor. He rolled toward the door that led from the dining-room to the kitchen, and, just as he reached it, Dinah came in with Mr. Bobbsey's cup of iced tea.

Before Freddie could stop himself, and before fat Dinah could get out of the way, the little Bobbsey chap had rolled right into the cook, and down she went in a heap on the floor, the cup and saucer crashing into dozens of pieces, and the tea spilling all over.

CHAPTER II

NEW SUMMER PLANS

"OH, Freddie!"

"Oh, Dinah!"

"Are you hurt?"

Thus came the cries, and as Snap, the dog, rushed in just then, barking and leaping about, he made the confusion all the worse.

Mr. Bobbsey sprang from his chair, lifted Freddie out of the way, and then helped Dinah to her feet. The fat, colored cook looked around in a dazed manner, and Freddie, too, did not seem to know just what had happened to him.

"Oh, don't tell me he is hurt—or Dinah, either!" cried Mrs. Bobbsey, holding her hands over her eyes, as though she might see something unpleasant.

"I—I'm not hurt," said Freddie, "but I—I'm all wet!"

"Bress yo' heart, honey lamb! I'se glad ob dat!" cried Dinah, as she wiped her face on her apron, for the tea had splashed on her.

"Are you all right, Dinah?" asked Mr. Bobbsey, setting Freddie down, for he had caught his little fat son up in his arms.

"Shuah, I'se all right, sah," the colored cook answered. "Jest shook up a bit. I'se so fat it doesn't hurt me t' fall," she explained. "An' I shuah am glad I didn't fall on Freddie. He done knocked mah feet right out from under me!"

"Yes, you shouldn't have turned somersaults in the house," said Mrs. Bobbsey. "That wasn't right, Freddie."

"I—I wasn't exactly turning somersaults," Freddie explained, as he dried his face in his pocket handkerchief. "I was jest rollin' over an' over, like I'm goin' to do down at Meadow Brook."

"Well, it was almost as bad as turning somersaults," said Nan. "My, but I got *so* excited."

"Pooh! It wasn't anything," spoke Bert. "It's a good thing, though, that it was iced tea, instead of being hot."

"Indeed that was a blessing," said Mrs. Bobbsey, while Dinah began picking up the pieces of the cup and saucer. "You must be more careful, Freddie."

"I will, ma," he promised. "But tell us about Meadow Brook. When can we go?"

"Not until you get a dry suit on, at least," said Mr. Bobbsey with a smile. "You had better change, Freddie. You are all wet from my cup of tea."

"I'll put dry things on him," offered Nan, leading the little fellow from the room. "But don't talk over any plans until I come back," she begged.

"We won't," promised her mother.

And while the house is settling into quietness, after the confusion of the temporary home-coming, and the upsetting of Dinah and Freddie, I will take just a few moments to tell my new readers something about the Bobbsey Twins as they have been written about in the other books of this series.

There were two sets of twins, and that may seem strange until I tell you that Bert and Nan, aged about nine, formed one set, and Flossie and Freddie, aged four years younger, made up the second set. Bert and Nan were tall and slim, with dark hair and eyes, while Flossie and Freddie were fat and short, with light hair and blue eyes, making a very different appearance from the older twins.

Besides the two sets of Bobbsey twins, there was Mr. Richard Bobbsey, and his wife Mary. They lived in an Eastern city called Lakeport, on Lake Metoka, where Mr. Bobbsey had a large lumber business.

I might say that Dinah Johnson, and her husband Sam, also formed part of the Bobbsey household, for without Dinah to cook, and without Sam to do everything around the house, from watering the grass to putting out the ashes, I do not know how Mrs. Bobbsey would have gotten along. And then, of course, there was Snoop, the black cat, and Snap, the nice dog, who had once been in a circus, and could do many tricks.

So much for the Bobbsey family. As for

what they did, if you will read the first book of the series, which volume is called "The Bobbsey Twins," you will get a good idea of the many good times Flossie, Freddie, Bert and Nan had.

Uncle Daniel Bobbsey, who was Mr. Bobbsey's brother, and his wife, Aunt Sarah, lived in the country at Meadow Brook Farm. They had a ten year old son, named Harry, and he and Bert were great chums whenever they were together.

The Bobbsey twins often went to the country, and also to the seashore, where their Uncle William and Aunt Emily, as well as their cousin Dorothy, lived, at a place called Ocean Cliff.

You may read of the fun the twins had at these places in the country and seashore books.

Bert, Nan, Flossie and Freddie also had fun at school, and when they went to Snow Lodge they had what were, to them, a wonderful series of adventures, and solved a strange mystery.

Their last trip had been on a houseboat. It was called the *Bluebird*, and they had voyaged down Lake Metoka to Lemby Creek, and through that to Lake Romano, where they had fine times. There was a mystery on the *Bluebird,* but Bert, and his cousin Harry, who was with him, found out what made the queer noises.

Cousin Dorothy was also a guest on the houseboat trip, and she and Nan, who were about the same age, greatly enjoyed themselves. The Bobbseys, and their country and seashore cousins, had come back from the trip, Dorothy going to her home, and Harry to his, when there happened the little accident to Freddie and Dinah, which I have mentioned in the first chapter of this book.

Now the house was quiet once again. Freddie had on a clean dry suit, Dinah had changed her damp apron for a fresh one, and Mr. Bobbsey was sipping his cup of iced tea, which was not spilled this time.

"Now can you tell us what we are going to do the rest of this summer vacation?" asked Bert.

"Yes," said Mr. Bobbsey, "I can. Your Uncle William, as I started to tell you, before

Freddie gave us that circus exhibition, has invited us up to Meadow Brook. And, as I have a little time I can spare from my business, I think I shall take you all down there. We can go to the country and have a fine time."

"We had a good time on the houseboat," said Nan. "It was lovely there."

"Indeed it was," agreed Mrs. Bobbsey.

"And when we found the ghost!" exclaimed Bert.

"Hush! You mustn't say ghost!" cautioned Mrs. Bobbsey, with a smile. "It wasn't a ghost, you know."

"Well, we thought it was—at first," laughed Bert. "Anyhow we'll have some fun at Meadow Brook."

"I'm going to fly a kite!" declared Freddie.

"All right, as long as you don't tie Snoop to the tail of it," said his father.

"And I'm going to feed the chickens," exclaimed Flossie.

"But you mustn't chase the rooster," cautioned her mother.

"I won't," promised the little fat twin.

"Now when are we going?" asked Nan.

"What train do we take?" Bert wanted to know.

"I'll have to see to all that to-morrow," said Mr. Bobbsey. "We might as well go right off to the country, for it is not very pleasant staying in the hot city. We won't need to unpack much, for we'll stay here only this one night. To-morrow morning we shall start for Meadow Brook."

"And are we going to take the *Bluebird* along?" inquired Flossie.

"No, the houseboat will stay at home this trip," her mother said. "There isn't enough water at Meadow Brook to sail the *Bluebird*."

They talked over their new summer plans, and the children were delighted at the prospect of going to see their cousin, their uncle and their aunt.

"Dinah is going, isn't she?" asked Nan.

"Oh, yes, we couldn't get along without her," answered Mrs. Bobbsey with a smile.

"And I'm going to take Snoop!" cried Freddie, hugging the big, black cat, which did not seem to mind being loved so hard.

"Well if Snoop goes, then we ought to take

Snap, the dog, too," declared Bert. "Snap would be lonesome if he were left behind, wouldn't he?"

"Oh, may we take them both, mamma?" begged Nan.

"Well, I guess so," was the answer, as Mrs. Bobbsey looked at her husband.

"That will be all right," he nodded. "The country is just the place for dogs and cats—it's better for them than houseboats."

"Oh, what fun we'll have!" sang Flossie. "What lovely times!"

"And I'm going to take my fire engine, and squirt water in it from the brook," declared Freddie.

"Well, be careful not to fall in," his father said. "And now I shall have to go back to the office again, to do a little work so as to get ready for going away again. So I'll leave my little fat fireman and fat fairy for a while," and he smiled at Freddie and Flossie, as he called them by their pet names.

As the Bobbseys were to leave town soon, they did not unpack very much from the valises they had brought from the houseboat.

This boat was tied up at a dock in the lumber yard, which was on the edge of the lake. The children spent the morning playing about in the yard, some of their friends, who had not gone away for the summer, coming to join in their games.

After lunch Mr. Bobbsey came up to the house in an automobile, bringing his wife some things she had asked him to get from the store.

"Oh, may I have a ride?" begged Freddie, when he saw his father in the machine, which Mr. Bobbsey and some of the other members of his lumber firm used when they were in a hurry.

"Yes, jump in!" invited his father. "Want to come, Bert?" he asked of the older Bobbsey boy.

"Yes, thank you," was the answer. "Where are you going?"

"I have to go up the lake shore, to a place called Tenbly, to see another lumber dealer on some business," Mr. Bobbsey said. "Where are Nan and Flossie?" he asked his wife, who had come out on the porch just then. "I could take them along also. There is plenty of room."

"Flossie and Nan have gone over to Mrs. Black's house," Mrs. Bobbsey said. "Run along without them. It's just as well. I'd rather they wouldn't be out in the hot sun, as we have to take a long train journey to-morrow."

"All right," agreed Mr. Bobbsey, as he started off in the automobile with Freddie and Bert. "We'll soon be back."

Neither Mr. Bobbsey nor the boys knew what was to happen on that ride, nor how it was to affect them afterward.

CHAPTER III

THE RUNAWAY BOY

It was a pleasant trip for Freddie and Bert to ride with their father in the automobile along the shady shores of the lake. The little twin, and the bigger one, sat back on the cushions, now and then bouncing up and down as the machine went over a rough place in the road.

Freddie, being lighter than Bert, bounced up and down oftener, but then he was so fat, almost "like a lump of butter," as his mother used to say, that he did not much mind it.

"I wish we could take this machine to Meadow Brook Farm with us," said Bert, as they neared the lumber yard of Mr. Mason, with whom Mr. Bobbsey had business that day.

"We can ride in one of Uncle Daniel's carriages," said Freddie. "Or maybe I can ride horse-back. That would be fun!" he cried, his bright eyes sparkling.

"It's fun—if you don't fall off," Bert said.

As the automobile passed around a curve in the road, where the lake could be seen stretching out its sparkling waters in the bright sun, Bert suddenly uttered a cry, and pointed ahead.

"Look!" he exclaimed. "There are two little girls drifting out in that boat, and they don't seem to know how to row to shore."

Mr. Bobbsey steered the machine down to the edge of the lake, over the grass at one side of the road. As he did so he and the two boys heard voices faintly calling:

"Help!! Help! Oh, somebody please come and get us!"

"I'll get them—I can row, and there's another boat on shore," said Bert, pointing to a craft drawn up on the sand.

"I guess I'd better go out—you stay with Freddie," directed the lumber merchant, as he brought the automobile to a stop, and jumped out.

"I'm coming!" he called to the two little girls in the drifting boat. "Don't be afraid, and sit still! Don't stand up!"

He needed to caution them thus, for one of

the girls, seeing that help was on the way, grew so excited that she stood up, and this is always dangerous to do in a rowboat on the water. Rowboats tip over very easily, and sometimes even good swimmers may be caught under them.

"I wish I could help get them," sighed fat Freddie, as he saw his father run down to the shore of the lake, and shove the other boat into the water.

"It's best to let papa do it," said Bert, though he himself would have liked to have gone to the rescue.

"They'll mind papa, and sit down and keep still, but they wouldn't mind us," went on Bert, explaining matters to his little brother.

"That's right," agreed Freddie. "Girls are awful 'fraid in a boat, anyhow. I'm not afraid."

"Well, not all girls are afraid, either," said Bert with a smile. "Nan isn't afraid."

"Of course not—she's our sister, and so is Flossie!" exclaimed Freddie, as if that made a difference!

Mr. Bobbsey was now rowing out to the two

small girls in the drifting boat. They did not seem to have any oars, and Bert and Freddie heard their father call to them again to sit down, so they would not tip over.

Then the lumber man reached the drifting craft, and carefully fastened it by a rope to the boat he was in.

"Now sit quietly and I'll pull you to shore," he said to the girls. "You must not come out in a boat all alone. Where is your home?"

"Up there," replied the older girl, pointing to a house back of the lake shore road. "We didn't mean to come out," she went on. "We just sat in the boat when it was tied fast to the dock, but the knot must have come loose, and we drifted out. We're ever so much obliged to you for coming out to us"

"Well, don't get in boats again, unless some older person is with you," cautioned Mr. Bobbsey. By this time he had towed the boat, with the girls in it, to shore. As he did so a woman came running from the house, calling out:

"Oh, what has happened? Oh, are they drowned?"

"Nothing at all has happened," said Mr.

Bobbsey, quietly. "Your children just drifted out, and I went and got them."

"Oh, and I've told them never, never to get into a boat!" cried the mother. "Girls, girls! What am I going to do to you?" she went on. "You might have fallen overboard."

"Yes, that is true, they might have," said Mr. Bobbsey. "But I think this will be a lesson to them, and no harm has come to them this time. But it is best for children to keep out of boats."

"Indeed it is," agreed the lady. "Oh, I can't thank you enough, sir!" she said to Mr. Bobbsey. "I have told Sallie and Jane never to go out on the lake unless Frank is with them, but he isn't here now."

"Is Frank their brother?" asked Mr. Bobbsey.

"Not exactly a brother. My husband is his guardian," the lady went on. "I am Mrs. Mason."

"Oh, I am glad to know you," said Mr. Bobbsey. "I am on my way to your husband's office now, to see him on business. I am glad I could do you a favor."

"Indeed it is more than a favor," said Mrs. Mason. "I cannot thank you enough. When Frank was home I did not worry so much about the girls, as he looked after them. But my husband thinks he is now old enough to help in the lumber yard, and so he keeps him down at the office. You are going down there, you say?"

"Yes," replied Mr. Bobbsey. "I am going along the river road."

"I can show you a shorter route," said Mrs. Mason, who now had tight hold of her daughters' hands, as though she feared they would run down to the boats again. "My husband has cut a new road through the orchard, down to his office," she went on. "You can come that way in your machine, and save nearly a mile."

"I shall be glad to do that," Mr. Bobbsey answered, "as I haven't very much time today. We are getting ready to go away."

Mrs. Mason showed Mr. Bobbsey where he could cross the main road, and take a short cut through an old orchard, to reach the lumber office, and soon, after waving good-bye to the frightened little girls, Mr. Bobbsey, Bert and Freddie were again on their way.

"Is—is the lake very deep where those girls were?" Freddie wanted to know.

"It doesn't make much difference whether it is deep or not," said Mr. Bobbsey, "they would probably have been drowned if they had fallen overboard. You must always be careful about boats," he cautioned the little fellow.

"I will," Freddie promised.

"That must be the lumber yard!" exclaimed Bert a little later, when they turned from the new orchard road into another highway.

"Yes, that is it," Mr. Bobbsey agreed. "I never came this way before. It is a good road to know when you are in a hurry."

Mr. Mason's lumber yard, like that of Mr. Bobbsey, was partly on the edge of the lake, so the logs, boards and planks could be easily loaded and unloaded from boats. Part of the yard was on the other side of the road, back from the lake, and it was on this side that the office was built.

As Mr. Bobbsey and his two boys rode up in the automobile, they saw out in front of the office a strange and not very pleasant sight. A man stood there, roughly shaking a boy about Bert's age. The boy seemed to be crying, and trying to get away, but the man held him tightly by one arm, and shook him again and again.

"I don't like that," said Mr. Bobbsey in a low voice, as he stopped the automobile.

"What makes him do it?" asked Freddie. "Is the boy bad?"

"I'll teach you to make me lose money that way!" cried the man as he again roughly shook the boy. "You ought to have better sense than to be cheated that way! It wasn't your money that you lost, it was mine, and money isn't so easily made these days!"

"But I couldn't help it!" the boy cried, trying to pull his arm away. He could not do this, for the man held it too tightly.

"Yes, you could help it too, if you'd had your eyes open!" the man said in harsh tones. "I left you in charge of the office, and you ought to have been sharp enough not to be fooled and cheated. I—I don't know what to do to you!"

Again he shook the boy.

"Ouch! You hurt, Mr. Mason!" cried the lad.

"Well, you deserve to be hurt, losing money that way," was the answer. "I—I've a good notion to——"

But the sentence was not finished. Just then, by a sudden motion, the boy pulled away from the man who was shaking him, and ran down the road. For a moment it seemed as if the man would run after him, but he did not. The two stood looking at one another, while Mr. Bobbsey, having alighted from the automobile, walked up toward the lumber office.

"You'd better come back here, Frank," called the man who had been shaking the boy. "You'd better come back."

"I'll never come back!" was the answer. "I—I'm going to run away! I'll never live with you again! You treat me too mean! It wasn't my fault about that bad money! I couldn't help it. I'm going to run away, and I'm never coming back again. I can't stand it here!"

Bursting into tears, the boy raced off down the road in a cloud of dust.

CHAPTER IV

OFF FOR MEADOW BROOK

LITTLE Freddie, who sat beside his older brother, Bert, in Mr. Bobbsey's automobile, looked on with wonder in his childish eyes, as he saw the boy Mr. Mason had been shaking run down the road.

"What's the matter with him, Bert?" Freddie asked. "Didn't he like to be shook?"

"I should say *not!*" exclaimed Bert. "And I wouldn't myself. I don't think that man did right to shake him so."

"It was too bad," added Freddie. "Say, Bert," he went on eagerly, "maybe we could catch up to him in the automobile, and we could take him to Meadow Brook with us. Nobody would shake him there."

"No, I guess they wouldn't," said Bert slowly, thinking how kind his uncle and aunt were.

"Then let's go after him!" begged Freddie.

"No, we couldn't do that, Freddie," Bert said with a smile at his little brother. "The boy maybe wouldn't want to come with us, and besides, papa wouldn't let me run the auto, though I know which handles to turn, for I've watched him," Bert went on, with a firm belief that he could run the big car almost as well as could Mr. Bobbsey.

"Well, when papa comes back I'm going to ask him to go after that boy and bring him with us," declared Freddie. "I don't like to see boys shook."

"I don't, either," murmured Bert.

By this time Mr. Bobbsey had come up to where Mr. Mason was standing.

"Oh, how do you do, Mr. Bobbsey," spoke the other lumber man. "I didn't expect to see you for some days."

"I did come a little ahead of time," went on the twins' father. "But I am going to take my family off to the country, so I thought I would come and see you, and finish up our business before going away."

"I'm always glad to talk business," Mr.

Mason said, "but I thought your folks were out somewhere on a houseboat."

"We were, and just came back to-day. But the summer isn't over, and we're going to my brother's place, at Meadow Brook Farm. But you seem to be having some trouble," he went on, nodding down the road in the direction the sobbing boy had run. "Of course it isn't any affair of mine, but——"

"Yes, trouble! Lots of it!" interrupted Mr. Mason bitterly. "I have had a lot of trouble with that boy."

"That's too bad," spoke Mr. Bobbsey. "He seems a bright sort of chap. He isn't your son, is he?"

"No, I'm his guardian. He's my ward. His father was a friend of mine in business, and when he died he asked me to look after the boy. His name is Frank Kennedy."

"Oh, yes, I heard about him," said Mr. Bobbsey.

"Heard about him! I guess you didn't hear any good then!" exclaimed the other lumber man, rather crossly. "What do you mean?"

"Why, we came past your house a little

while ago," said Mr. Bobbsey, "and your wife mentioned a Frank Kennedy who used to take your two daughters out rowing. If he had been there to-day the girls probably wouldn't have gone out alone, and drifted away."

"Drifted away! What do you mean?" cried Mr. Mason. "Has anything happened?"

"It's all right, my papa went out in a boat and got 'em!" cried Freddie in his shrill, childish voice, for he heard what his father and Mr. Mason were saying.

"I—I don't understand," said the other lumber dealer, seriously. "Was there an accident?"

"Oh, it wasn't anything," Mr. Bobbsey said. "When I went past your house, near the river, I saw the two girls adrift in a boat, not far from shore. They had floated out while playing. I went after them and your wife, before she showed me this short cut to your place, spoke about an adopted boy, Frank Kennedy, who used to play with the children."

"Oh, I'm much obliged to you," said Mr. Mason, after a pause. "Yes, Frank did look after the girls some. That was he who just ran down the road. But he did better at home than he's doing in my office.

"What do you mean?" asked Mr. Bobbsey, wondering why it was that Mr. Mason had so severely shaken the boy who had run away.

"Well, I mean that Frank just lost twenty dollars for me," proceeded the lumber man.

"Twenty dollars! How was that?" asked Mr. Bobbsey.

"I left him in charge of my office, while I was out on some other business," went on the lumber dealer, "and a strange man came in and bought two dollars worth of expensive boards. Frank gave them to him, and the man took them away with him, as they were not very large, or heavy to carry.."

"Two dollars—I thought you said twenty!" exclaimed Mr. Bobbsey.

"So I did. Wait until I tell you all. As I said, Frank sold this strange man two dollars worth of boards. The man gave Frank a twenty dollar bill, and Frank gave him back eighteen dollars in change."

"Well, wasn't that right?" asked Mr. Bobbsey, with a smile. "Two dollars from twenty leave eighteen—or it used to when I went to school."

"That part is all right," Mr. Mason said, bitterly, "but the fact is that the twenty dollar bill Frank took from the strange man is no good. It is bad money, and no one but a child would take it. It's a bill that was gotten out by the Confederate states during the Civil War, and of course their money isn't any better than waste-paper now. I don't see how Frank was fooled that way. I wouldn't have been if I had been in the office."

"Perhaps the boy never saw a Confederate bill before," suggested Mr. Bobbsey.

"No matter, he should have known that it wasn't good United States' money!" declared Mr. Mason. "By his carelessness to-day he lost me twenty dollars; the eighteen dollars in my good money that he gave the man in change, and the two dollars worth of boards. And all I have to show for it is that worthless piece of paper!" and Mr. Mason took from his pocket a crumpled bill.

Mr. Bobbsey looked at it carefully.

"Yes, that's one of the old Confederate

States' bills all right," he said, "and it isn't worth anything, except as a curiosity."

"It cost me twenty dollars, all right," said Mr. Mason, with a sour look on his face. "I can't see how Frank was so foolish as to be taken in by it."

"Well, the poor boy knew no better, and probably he is sorry enough now," said Mr. Bobbsey.

"I guess he's sorry enough!" exclaimed Mr. Mason, bitterly. "I gave him a good shaking, as he is too big to whip. I shook him and scolded him."

"Well, almost anyone, not very familiar with money, might have made that mistake," spoke Mr. Bobbsey. "This Confederate bill looks very much like some of ours, and a person in a hurry might have been fooled by it."

"Oh, nonsense!" broke in Mr. Mason. "There was no excuse for Frank being fooled as he was. "I won't listen to any such talk! He lost me twenty dollars and he'll have to make it up to me, somehow."

"But how can he, when he has run away?" asked Mr. Bobbsey, and he felt very sorry for

Frank, who was not much older than Bert. Mr. Bobbsey knew how grieved he would be if something like that happened to his son.

"Yes, he pretended to run away," said Mr. Mason, "but he'll soon run back again."

"How do you know?" Mr. Bobbsey wanted to know. "Did he ever run away before?"

"No, he never did," admitted Mr. Mason, "but he'll have to run back because he has nowhere to run to. He can't get anything to eat, he has no money, and he can't find a place to sleep. Of course he'll come back!

"And when he does come back," Mr. Mason went on, "I'll make him work doubly hard to pay back that twenty dollars. I can't afford to lose that much money."

"But it was an accident; a mistake that anyone might have made," said Mr. Bobbsey again.

"Nonsense!" cried the other lumber man. "I'll make Frank Kennedy pay for his mistake!"

"Perhaps the strange man did not mean to give him the Confederate bill," went on Bert's father. "Some persons carry those old South ern bills as souvenirs, or pocket-pieces, and this man might have paid his out by mistake. I know that once happened to me with a piece of money. He may come back and give you a good twenty dollar bill."

"I am not so foolish as to hope anything like that will happen," said Mr. Mason. "No, I'm out twenty good hard-earned dollars. That's all there is to it. But I'll get it out of Frank Kennedy, somehow."

"If he ever comes back," said Mr. Bobbsey, in a low voice.

"Oh, he'll come back—never fear!" responded the other lumber dealer. Mr. Bobbsey gently shook his head. He was not so sure of that. Frank, as he ran down the road, crying, seemed to feel very badly indeed, and when he said he would never come back it sounded as though he meant it.

"Poor little chap!" thought Mr. Bobbsey to himself. "I am very sorry for him. I wonder where he will sleep to-night?" And he could not help thinking how badly he would feel if he knew his own two dear boys had to be without a place to sleep, or somewhere to get a meal.

Mr. Mason did not appear to worry about the plight of his ward, for whom he was guardian.

The lumber dealers finished their business and Mr. Mason again thanked Mr. Bobbsey for what he had done for the two girls in the boat.

"I guess I'd better keep Frank at the house after this," went on Mr. Mason. "He's safer there than at the office, and wouldn't lose me so much money. But I'll get it out of him, some way," and he thrust back into his pocket the bad twenty dollar bill.

Bert had understood most of the talk between his father and Mr. Mason, but little Freddie did not know much of what went on except that Frank had run away.

"I wouldn't run away from my home," he said. "I like it too much."

"Yes, but you haven't anyone at your home to shake you as hard as that man did," said Bert. "I don't blame Frank for running away."

"Poor boy!" sighed Mr. Bobbsey. "Life is a hard matter for a little chap with no real home."

In the automobile the lumber man and his two boys went back to Lakeport, passing on their way the house where Mr. Mason lived. The two little girls waved their hands to Freddie and Bert as the boys rode past. But there was no sign of Frank Kennedy.

The sadness of the scene the two Bobbsey boys had witnessed was soon forgotten in the joys of getting ready to go to Meadow Brook. They spent that night in their city house, unpacking only such few things as they needed. When morning came Flossie and Freddie were the first up.

"We're going to the country!" sang Flossie, walking about in a long night-gown that trailed over the floor.

"Going to Meadow Brook!" chanted Freddie. "Where's Snoop? I'm going to take him!"

"And may we take Snap, too?" asked Bert, who had taught the former circus dog many new tricks.

"Yes, we'll take them both," said Mrs. Bobbsey. "Now hurry, children dear. We are going to leave soon after breakfast, and it is a long ride in the train, you know."

"Are we going to ride in the 'merry-go-round car'?" asked Flossie.

"She means a parlor car, with chairs that swing around," said Nan, with a laugh.

"Yes, we'll ride in a chair car," decided Mr. Bobbsey.

The Bobbsey house was soon a very busy place. Valises that had been opened were packed again. Dinah got a quick breakfast. Mr. Bobbsey had much telephoning to do about business matters, and Mrs. Bobbsey—well, she had to do what all mothers do on such occasions—look after everything. Nan and Bert helped as much as they could.

Flossie and Freddie tried to help, but you know how it is with little children. The two smaller twins were very anxious that Snoop, the black cat, be taken with them in his little traveling crate.

"I'll get him and pack him up," said Freddie.

"And I'll help," offered Flossie.

Soon all was in readiness for the start to the depot where the Bobbseys would take the train for Meadow Brook. Just as the automobile came up to the door to take the family, there arose a cry from the direction of the side porch where Flossie and Freddie had gone with the cat-cage, in which to put Snoop.

"Oh, my!" exclaimed Mrs. Bobbsey. "I wonder what has happened now? I hope those twins are all right!"

"I'll go see!" offered Nan, setting off on a run.

CHAPTER V

SNAP'S ESCAPE

NAN found Flossie and Freddie, standing one on either side of the wooden crate in which Snoop made his journeys. The twins each had hold of the black cat, who did not seem to be enjoying life very much just then.

"He goes in this way, I tell you!" shouted Freddie.

"No, he goes in the other way!" cried Flossie, and then they both tried, at the same time, to thrust poor Snoop into his cage.

The cat cried out, and scrambled to get away.

"What's the matter?" asked Nan. "What does all this mean, Flossie and Freddie? Don't you know the automobile is waiting to take us to the station?"

"Well, I want to put Snoop in his cage!" insisted Freddie.

"And so do I!" cried Flossie.

"But she—she—Flossie wants to put him in, tail end first!" went on the excited little boy.

"Course—'cause that's right!" went on the little girl. "Freddie says he ought to go in head first," she exclaimed, "and you know, Nan, if you stand Snoop on his head he'll get dizzy, like I did when I hung dingle-dangle by my legs from the swing."

"And if he goes in tail first he'll get all tangled up!" retorted Freddie, who was almost crying now.

"Oh, dear!" exclaimed Nan. "I guess I'll have to call papa or mamma, and they have enough to look after as it is, with the auto here, and almost train time. I never saw such children! What am I to do?"

"Let me put Snoop in tail first!" cried Flossie.

"No, he ought to go in his box head first!" declared her brother, and neither one of them would let go of the black cat. Snoop looked sadly at Nan, as though he wished she would rescue him, and put him in the traveling box either end first, if only he might be left in peace and quietness.

"Oh, dear!" Nan exclaimed again. "I really don't know what to do! I guess we'll leave Snoop home altogether!"

"Oh, no!" cried Flossie and Freddie.

"Here! What's all the trouble?" asked Bert, running around to the side porch. "Hurry up! The auto is waiting."

"It's these twins!" said Nan, hopelessly.

"It's Flossie!" accused Freddie. "She wants Snoop to go in tail end first, and he'll get all tangled up, 'cause he's got an awful long tail."

"And Freddie wants to put him in head first, and he'll get dizzy same as I did in the swing!" accused Flossie.

"Here! I'll settle this!" cried Bert, like a manly little chap. "Give me that cat!"

He took Snoop from Flossie and Freddie, who let go willingly enough. If Snoop could have talked he would have said, "Thank you, Bert!" I am sure he would have.

"There, we'll put him in feet first," Bert went on, carefully lowering the black cat into the box that way. "A cat always likes to land feet first," he explained. "then he won't get tangled up in his tail, nor dizzy. Now, Flossie and Freddie, hustle around front and get into the auto. I'll bring Snoop" he continued, as he fastened down the lid of the traveling cage.

"That's right! Feet first!" cried Freddie, a happy smile on his face.

"Of course! Why didn't we think of putting Snoop in that way?" asked Flossie, as she put her chubby hand in her brother's and ran with him around to the front porch.

"Oh, such children!" sighed Nan as she followed Bert, who carried Snoop in his cage. The black cat curled up and went to sleep. He was used to traveling this way.

"My! What was the trouble?" asked Mrs. Bobbsey. Nan and Bert explained, while Flossie and Freddie took their places in the gasoline machine.

"Are you all ready?" asked Mr. Bobbsey. "How about you, Dinah?" for the colored cook was being taken to the country to help look after the smaller twins.

"Oh, indeedy I'se all right, Mrs. Bobbsey."

was Dinah's answer. "Heah, Freddie, let ole Dinah carry dat cat-box," for Bert had given Snoop in his cage to the small twin boy.

"No, I want to hold him," Freddie insisted, and he was allowed to have his way.

Sam, Dinah's husband, was to stay home to look after the Bobbsey city house, and he waved a good-bye as the automobile started off.

"Where's Snap?" asked Flossie, as they were rolling down the street.

"He's coming," reported Nan, for the big dog was running alongside the car. There would have been room for him to ride in it, but he preferred racing along the street, and he would be at the depot waiting for the family when they arrived.

"The train will be here in about five minutes," said Mr. Bobbsey, after they had reached the depot, and he had purchased the tickets. Then, while Flossie and Freddie took turns looking in at black Snoop through the slats of the box, Nan and Bert helped gather the valises into one pile. Mr. Bobbsey went to see about getting the trunks checked, and also about sending Snap in the baggage car, for the dog would have to ride that way to Meadow Brook.

At last, with a toot of the whistle, and a ringing of the bell, the engine, drawing the train, puffed into the station.

"All aboard!" called the conductor.

Many persons were getting on, while others were getting off. Mr. Bobbsey gathered his little family down toward the parlor, or chair, car.

"Heah you am, sah!" exclaimed the colored porter as he swung Flossie and Freddie up the steps, and helped Mrs. Bobbsey and Dinah. Nan and Bert felt big enough not to need any help.

"Hello! What's dish yeah?" cried the porter, as he picked up the box containing Snoop. "Am dish good to eat?" he asked, looking in at the black cat. "What am it?"

"Oh, it's our Snoop!" cried Flossie. "Don't hurt him!"

"'Deed an' I won't, little Missie!" laughed the colored porter. "I thought maybe it was a watermelon yo' all had in dat box."

"All aboard!" called the conductor again, and then, with the Bobbseys safely in their chair car, the train puffed away again, going faster and faster.

"The engine can hardly get its breath," remarked Freddie, as he listened to the puffing of the locomotive.

"I guess it's going up hill," said Bert, with a laugh.

The ride to Meadow Brook would take nearly all day, and Mrs. Bobbsey settled herself comfortably in the easy chair to look out of the window, after she had seen that Flossie and Freddie were all right. Nan and Bert looked after themselves, and Mr. Bobbsey, having seen that his family was comfortable, began to read his paper. Dinah took a chair in one corner where she could doze off. It always made her sleepy to ride in a train, she said.

Nan and Bert looked out at the passing scenery, as did Flossie and Freddie, when they were not taking turns peeking in at Snoop. As for the black cat himself, he had curled up into a little round ball, and was fast asleep.

He had become a traveler by this time, for once he had been to Cuba, when the circus lady took him, as I told you in one of the other books.

"I wonder how Snap is getting along in the baggage car?" said Bert to Nan, after a bit. "I think I'll go in and see."

"Oh, will papa let you?" inquired his sister.

"I don't know. I'll ask him."

Mr. Bobbsey was a little doubtful about letting Bert pass from one car to another when the train was moving.

"But it's a vestibule train, papa," said the boy. "It's like one big car. I can't fall off."

"Well, I don't know," said Mr. Bobbsey, slowly.

"I'll take him up front, if he wants to see about the dog," said a brakeman who had heard Bert's talk.

"Oh, thank-you," said Mr. Bobbsey. "Be careful, Bert."

But, as it turned out, there was no danger at all. As Bert had said, the cars were joined together with "vestibules," that made the train like one big railway coach. And as it was slowing up to stop at a station, when Bert went forward to the baggage car, he had no trouble at all in walking along with the brakeman.

Bert found Snap very glad indeed to see him, and as the train was then at a standstill the boy took the chain off the dog's collar, and let him run about the car a little, for he had to be kept chained fast while the cars were in motion.

"I guess you want to run about a bit, eh, Snap?" said Bert.

"Bow wow!" barked the dog, and that was the best answer he could make. The man in the baggage car had seen to it that Snap had plenty of water to drink, for the day was very hot.

"Better chain him up again, my boy," suggested the baggage man, after a bit. "We'll start pretty soon now."

Bert led Snap over to the side of the car, where the collar-chain dangled, but, just then, Snap, looking out of the door of the baggage car, saw a strange dog on the depot platform. Whether Snap knew this dog, or thought he did, Bert could not tell.

But, an instant later, with a bark, Snap pulled away from Bert's grasp on his collar, and leaped out of the open car door. At the same moment the train started off.

"Snap! Snap!" cried Bert. "Come back here!"

CHAPTER VI

AT MEADOW BROOK

THE train was not going very fast when Snap leaped from the baggage car, but, even if it had been moving at greater speed, it is not likely that Snap would have been hurt.

As it was, when the dog leaped from the open door, he did a somersault in the air, for he had learned to do that while in the circus, when he jumped from a high place.

"Snap! Snap!" called Bert again.

But Snap landed lightly on his feet, and raced across the depot platform toward the dog he had seen.

"Say, that's a fine dog of yours!" cried the baggage man admiringly to Bert. "He must be a trick one."

"He is!" answered Bert. "But can I get him back again? Oh, I must get him!" and he looked about for some way to do this.

"Don't jump out, whatever you do!" warned the brakeman who had brought Bert to the baggage car. The man stood in front of the open door, out of which trunks were taken. But Bert had no idea of doing what Snap had done. Besides, the train was moving quite rapidly now.

"Oh, how can I get my dog back?" Bert wanted to know.

"You can telegraph back, from the next station we stop at, and have the agent there send him on, wherever you are going," explained the baggage man.

"Oh, but we're going a long way," Bert said. "I'm afraid Snap would be lost, traveling alone. Oh, what will Nan say!"

Nan was as fond of Snap as was Bert himself, though perhaps the smaller twins, Flossie and Freddie cared more for Snoop, the black cat. But of course they loved Snap very much.

Poor Bert did not know what to do. Just then his father came running into the car.

"Did Snap get away?" cried Mr. Bobbsey. "Your mother saw a dog on the station platform that looked like him," went on the lumber man to Bert. "Is Snap——"

"He's gone!" interrupted Bert. "He jumped out of the car just now, and——"

"We must stop the train!" Mr. Bobbsey explained.

"All right, I guess we can make up any time we lose," the brakeman said. He reached up and pulled the cord that ran overhead in the car. There was a hissing of air, the locomotive whistle blew sharply, and the train came slowly to a stop. The brakeman had pulled an air whistle in the engine cab, and the engineer, hearing it, and knowing the train ought to stop, had turned off the steam.

Mr. Bobbsey then went to the door of the baggage car, and, leaning out, whistled in a way Snap well knew. He could see the dog, back on the depot platform, "wagging tails" with another dog.

"Here, Snap! Snap!" called Mr. Bobbsey, as the train slowly came to a stop. "Here Snap!"

Bert leaned out beside his father, and also whistled and called. Then Snap knew he had done wrong to jump out, and back he came, racing as hard as he could.

"I'll open the end door of the car if you wish, so he can come up the steps," offered the brakeman.

"You don't need to, thank you," replied Mr. Bobbsey. "I guess Snap can jump up here, though it is pretty high."

By this time a number of persons from the train had either gotten out, or thrust their heads from the windows, to learn the reason for the sudden stop. But when they saw the dog they understood.

"Up, Snap! Up!" called Mr. Bobbsey, as the children's pet came leaping along beside the track. Snap gave one look up at the high sill of the baggage car door, and then, with a loud bark, he gave a great leap and landed right beside Bert.

"Say, that dog's a fine jumper!" cried several railroad men who had come up to see what the trouble was.

"Yes, he is a pretty good dog, nearly always," Mr. Bobbsey said, "but he made trouble for us to-day. Now, Snap, you'll have to stay chained up the rest of the trip, until we get to Meadow Brook."

Snap would not like that, Bert knew, but nothing else could be done. The train soon started off again, and when Bert and his father went back to the parlor car where the rest of the family were riding they told all that had happened.

"Snoop is better than Snap," said Freddie as he listened to the story.

"Yes, indeed," agreed his sister Flossie. "Snoop wouldn't jump out of a train and make a lot of trouble."

"Well, he did run away, once," declared Nan, who did not like to hear Snap talked about.

"Besides, Snoop is fast in a box, and he couldn't get out if he wanted to," added Bert, with a laugh.

So the children talked about their pets, now and then looking out of the windows at the scenery, while Dinah dozed off in her chair, and Mr. and Mrs. Bobbsey spoke of different matters.

Bert heard something of what his father and

mother were saying, and once he heard mentioned the name of Frank Kennedy.

"That's the boy who ran away from Mr. Mason, the lumber man," said Bert to himself. "I wonder what became of him, and if we'll ever see poor Frank again?"

And he little thought how soon, and under what circumstances, he was to meet the unfortunate lad again.

One of the porters, wearing a white cap, jacket and apron walked through the chair car about noon, calling out:

"First call fo' dinner in de dinin' car! First call fo' dinner!"

"Do they eat on trains?" asked Flossie.

"Yes, and at cute little tables," said Nan.

"Did we eat at them the last time we went to Meadow Brook?" Freddie wanted to know.

"No, you were too little then," said Mrs. Bobbsey, "and we brought our lunch with us. But this time we shall go to the diner."

"Oh, what fun!" cried Flossie.

Mr. Bobbsey led the way for his family into the dining-coach. As Nan had said, there were cute little tables against the side of the car, and on each table was a little dish of ferns, and other green plants, making a pretty decoration.

Dinah would not come. She said she would rather eat some chicken sandwiches she had in her bag, and Mr. Bobbsey let the dear old colored cook do as she pleased.

The Bobbsey twins found it so strange to eat in a car, at a real table, while rushing along, that I think they did not eat as much as they would have done at home. But they enjoyed it just the same, though Freddie did splash some water from his finger bowl on the table cloth.

"Oh! Oh!" he exclaimed when he saw what he had done. He looked anxiously at his mother.

"Dat's all right, little man," said the colored waiter with a smile that showed all his white teeth. "Got t' put a clean cloth on anyhow, an' watah doesn't matter."

Freddie felt better then.

The afternoon passed slowly enough. Mr. Bobbsey and Bert went to the baggage car once more, to see about Snap, but they found he was all right, having made friends with one of the men who looked after the travelers' trunks.

Nan read a story book which her mother bought from the train boy, and Flossie and Freddie did what Dinah was doing—took a little nap.

The train was due to arrive at Meadow Brook about five o'clock, and Mr. Bobbsey's brother, Uncle Daniel, was to meet the family at the station.

"Ours is the next stop," said the twins' papa, after a while. "Get your things together now."

"Oh, I had a fine sleep!" cried Freddie, stretching his chubby little arms.

"So did I," added Flossie. "I wonder if Snoop slept any?"

"I guess that's all he has been doing since we started," Mrs. Bobbsey answered. "He's all curled up into a black ball."

Flossie and Freddie looked at their pet, and Snoop stretched, and opened his mouth very wide, sticking out his red tongue.

"My! What a lot of teeth Snoop has!" cried Flossie.

"Did we bring his tooth brush?" asked Freddie.

"Cats don't have tooth brushes!" said Flossie.

"Their tongue is their tooth brush," explained Mrs. Bobbsey. "Did you ever feel how rough a cat's tongue is?"

"I never did!" said Flossie. "I'm going to feel now," and she knelt down on the carpeted floor of the car, and tried to get Snoop to put his red tongue out between the bars of the box.

"Oh, we haven't time for that now," said Mrs. Bobbsey. "Get ready to leave the train, Flossie."

Bundles and valises were gotten together, and, a little later, with a screeching of the brakes on the wheels, the train pulled slowly into the Meadow Brook station.

"I see Uncle Daniel!" cried Nan, looking from a window.

"Yes, and there's Harry!" cried Bert, as he spied his country cousin. "Oh, how glad I am!"

"Well, well! How are you all!" laughed Uncle Daniel as he hugged and kissed the two sets of twins. "My, but I'm glad to see you all!" he cried. "Welcome to Meadow Brook!"

"And we're glad to be here!" said Mrs. Bobbsey. "How is Aunt Sarah?"

"Just as fine as can be!" said her husband. "Now I have the same big wagon I had when you were here before. There's room for everybody in it, and all your baggage, too. Where's Dinah? You didn't leave her home, I hope!"

"No, indeedy! I'se heah!" exclaimed the fat, colored cook, who was carrying many bundles.

"Oh, we must get Snap out of the baggage car, before the train carries him away," said Mr. Bobbsey, and he hurried to do that, while his brother, Uncle Daniel, helped the boys and girls and Mrs. Bobbsey into the big wagon from the Bobbsey farm. The wagon had seats running along the side and was very comfortable to ride in.

Mr. Bobbsey soon came back with Snap, who was bouncing about, barking and wagging his tail, so glad was he to be among his friends again.

"Well, are you all ready to start?" asked

Uncle Daniel, as I shall call him, to distinguish him from Mr. Bobbsey, who was the farmer's brother.

"All ready, I think," answered Mrs. Bobbsey. And off they started for Meadow Brook farm, the horses prancing through the village streets.

"We'll have a lot of fun," said Harry to Bert, the two boys sitting next each other. "Maybe not as much fun as we had on your houseboat, Bert, but some, anyhow."

"I'm sure we shall," Bert said. "I like a farm just as much as I do a houseboat," he added politely.

"Have you got any little calves, Uncle Daniel?" asked Freddie.

"Yes," answered the farmer.

"And are there any little lambs?" Flossie wanted to know.

"Yes, but there's an old ram, too, and you want to look out that he doesn't chase you, and knock you down," Mr. Bobbsey's brother went on.

"Oh, is the ram dangerous?" asked Mrs. Bobbsey. quickly

"Oh, no!" her brother-in-law informed her. "His horns are so curved that he can't use the sharp points, but he just does love to come up behind and butt you down. He did it to me the other day. But I keep the ram in a pasture by himself."

The wagon rolled along the shady road, under the green trees, which made a grateful shade, for it was hot even though it was late in the afternoon.

"Oh, there is Tom Mason!" cried Bert, as he saw a country boy he had met when on a visit to Meadow Brook some time before. He waved his hand to Tom who was in his front yard, his house not being far from Mr. Bobbsey's.

"And there's Mabel Herold!" added Nan, as she saw a country girl she knew. "My, how she has grown!" Nan went on. "She didn't use to be up to my shoulder, and now she is taller than I am."

"Oh, the country is a great place for growing," Uncle Daniel said, with a chuckle.

"Mabel and Tom have been counting on your coming," said Harry. "I told them we expected you. We'll have some fine times together!"

"I'm sure of it," agreed Bert.

"Here we are!" called Uncle Daniel a little later, as the horses turned up a driveway in front of the Bobbsey country home. Lines of boxwood hedge grew along the graveled drive, and back of this hedge were beds of beautiful flowers, the perfume of which could be smelled this warm, August day.

"Oh, how lovely it is here," sighed Nan, turning around from having waved a welcome to Mabel Herold.

"Yes, I always like to come to Meadow Brook," said Mrs. Bobbsey.

"Whoa!" called Uncle Daniel.

The door of the house opened, and in it stood Aunt Sarah, and behind her Martha, the smiling servant.

"Oh, how glad I am to see you!" cried Aunt Sarah, as the children piled down from the wagon to hug and kiss her. "Now get your things off, and we'll have supper," she went on.

"I'm hungry!" announced Freddie.

"So am I!" added Flossie. "There was so

much to look at in that eating car, I didn't eat half enough.

"Well, we have plenty here, my dear," said her aunt.

"We must let Snoop out. I guess she's hungry, too," said Freddie, who never forgot the black cat. Snap, the dog, had raced along beside the wagon, and was now cooling his thirst at the spring near the side door.

The Bobbsey visitors were out on the shady porch, having laid aside their traveling wraps, and Uncle Daniel was coming down from the barn, having put away the horses, when a man rushed up the gravel drive, crying:

"Oh, Mr. Bobbsey! Mr. Bobbsey! He's out! He's loose!"

"Who's out? Who's loose?" the twins' uncle wanted to know.

"That old big ram! He's loose, and he's coming this way!" was the answer.

CHAPTER VII

THE PICNIC

THE man who had brought the news about the runaway ram, stood on the gravel drive near the porch, breathing hard, for he had run very fast to give the warning. He caught his breath, and then said again:

"The old ram is loose! He butted down the fence and got out. He's headed this way. What'll we do?"

"Children! Into the house with you—quick!" cried Mrs. Bobbsey.

"Oh! Oh!" cried Flossie. "Let me hide! Let me hide!"

"Pooh! I'm not afraid of a ram!" declared Freddie. "If I had my fire engine unpacked, I'd squirt water on him!"

"Better not try that, little fat fireman," said his father with a laugh. "Into the house with you, son. Your mother will look after you."

Nan had already started from the porch, leading Flossie, who kept looking back over her shoulder. From behind the hedge came a cry that sounded like:

"Baa! Baa! Baa!"

"There he comes!" exclaimed Nan. "Come on in, Bert and Harry," she begged the two boy cousins, who were peering eagerly down the road.

"I'm going to watch 'em catch him," said Bert.

"Better not let him see you," advised Harry. the country cousin. "That old ram is a hard hitter."

"Is there really any danger?" asked Mr. Bobbsey of his farmer-brother.

"Well, the old ram is pretty rough, I must say," answered Uncle Daniel, "and most of the men on the farm are afraid of him."

"He's coming right this way, I tell you!" exclaimed the hired man who had brought the news.

"Why should he head this way?" asked Mr. Bobbsey.

"Come along and I'll tell you," his brother

promised. "You children had better go into the house," he advised. "Yes, you too, Bert and Harry," he went on, as he saw his own son and Bert following him and Mr. Bobbsey. "No telling what notions old Upsetter will take."

"Is his name Upsetter?" asked Bert.

"It is," replied his uncle. "I call him that because he upsets so many things. He used to be a pet when he was little," he continued, "and that's what makes him come to the house now, whenever he gets loose. My wife got in the habit of feeding him salt, which all sheep like very much. I guess he must remember that. But Aunt Sarah wouldn't dare salt him now. Go back into the house, boys, and we men folks will look after the ram."

The sounds were nearer now:

"Baa! Baa! Baa!"

"Oh, he's coming!" cried Flossie, who stood with her nose pressed flat against a window near the porch.

"Had we better go in?" asked Bert of Harry.

"We really had," answered his cousin.

Uncle Daniel, Mr. Bobbsey and the hired man found some heavy sticks with which to scare the ram if he came too close. The big sheep was not yet in sight, though he could be heard bleating.

"Up this way," directed Uncle Daniel. "We can head him off and drive him into the barnyard, perhaps. Then I can shut him up until I have the fence mended that he knocked down."

"Why not get some salt for him?" suggested Mr. Bobbsey. "If he gets some to eat it may make him gentle, and then you could slip a rope around him and tie him up."

"That's a good idea!" cried the farmer. "Sam, please go to the house and get some salt," he directed.

Before the hired man returned, the ram had run into the driveway leading to the barn. Just as Uncle Daniel had said, the ram was headed for the house, which he must have remembered as a pleasant place ever since the days when he was a baby lamb. But now the ram was big and strong, and not very good-natured.

He stood for a moment, looking at Uncle Daniel, Mr. Bobbsey and the hired man. Then, pawing the ground with his fore feet, and lowering and shaking his head with its big horns, the ram started forward again.

"Oh, he's going to butt papa!" cried Flossie, who could see, from the window, what was going on.

"Papa will get out of the way, dear," said Mrs. Bobbsey. "Don't worry."

On came the ram, and then Uncle Daniel, taking the salt from the hired man, scattered some of it on the ground in front of the big sheep."

"That will stop him, I think," said the farmer. And indeed it did. Sheep, and all cattle, are very fond of licking up salt from the ground, and they will go a long way to find it. It keeps cattle healthy. The old ram, as soon as he smelled the salt, began licking it up with his tongue.

He paid no more attention to the men standing in front of him, though if the salt had not been there he probably would have run at them, and knocked them down with his big curved horns.

"Now's our chance!" whispered Mr. Bobbsey, as if the ram could understand what was said. "Get a rope and we can tie him up."

"I'll get one," offered the hired man, and when he came back with the clothes line Uncle Daniel made a loop in one end, such as the cowboys on the Western plains make when they lasso cattle.

And while the ram was busy licking up the salt, Uncle Daniel tossed the noose of the rope around the sheep's head, and, in another second, he and Mr. Bobbsey pulled it tight.

"Oh, they've caught him! They've caught him!" cried Nan, who stood near Flossie at the window.

"Come on out and look at him!" said Bert.

"No, no!" objected his mother, as the two boy cousins started from the room.

"Oh, I guess there's no danger now, if they have a rope on him," said Aunt Sarah.

"I'll go 'long with you," offered Freddie, "and I'd squirt water on that ram from my fire engine—if I had it unpacked."

"You stay right here with me," advised his mother, putting her arms around him.

Bert and Harry went out to look at the captured ram. The animal was not ugly now. Perhaps the salt made him good-natured. And he was soon led away, and tied up in a stable until his pasture fence could be mended.

"My! What a lot of excitement!" exclaimed Nan, when it was all over. "Nothing like this happened when we were on the houseboat."

"You forget the make-believe ghost," said Harry, with a laugh, for he had helped solve that mystery.

"Oh, that's so," agreed Nan. "That was exciting for a while."

The Bobbsey twins, as well as their father and mother, to say nothing of Dinah, were so tired from their long railroad journey that they went to bed early that night. The sun was shining brightly when they awakened next morning. Harry and Bert slept in the same room, and when the country boy arose from bed he went to the window to look out.

"Oh, dear! The sun's shining!" he exclaimed.

"Well, isn't that a good thing?" Bert wanted to know.

"Maybe," admitted Harry. "But if it had been raining we might have gone fishing. As it is, I shall have to work."

"What doing?" Bert wanted to know.

"Help pick apples in the orchard. We are shipping them away this year, and they have to be picked, and packed in barrels."

"I'll help you," offered Bert, and, after breakfast, the two boys went out to the big orchard, where Uncle Daniel and some of his men already were busy.

The apples were picked by men standing on long ladders that reached up into the trees. Each filled a canvas bag with apples. These bags hung around their necks, and when one was full, the man came down the ladder with it. This was so the apples would not be bruised, for a bruised apple rots very quickly, and even one rotten apple in a barrel full, will soon make many bad ones.

"Can we pick apples on a ladder?" asked Bert.

"No, that's a little too dangerous for small boys." said Uncle Daniel. "But you and Harry may pick those you can reach from the ground. Some of the tree limbs are very low, and you won't have any trouble. Take some of the bags to put the apples in. Don't bruise them."

Harry and Bert were soon busy, picking off as many apples as they could reach. When their bags were filled, they emptied them carefully in a wooden bin, and from that bin Uncle Daniel sorted the apples into barrels, which were "headed up" ready to be taken to the city.

Nan had gone over to the home of Mabel Herold, the country girl, and Flossie and Freddie found many things to amuse them about the farm. Later on they came out to the orchard, and picked up apples from the ground.

"I'll help fill Bert's bag, and you can help Harry," said Freddie to Flossie.

"No, little fat fireman," said Harry, using the pet name his uncle called Freddie. "The apples on the ground are called 'windfalls.' The wind blows them down, and they get crushed and bruised by falling on the hard dirt, or stones. It would not do to put them in with the good hand-picked apples."

"But what do you do with all those on the ground?" asked Bert, for there were a great many of them.

"Send them to the cider-mill, or feed them to the pigs," said Harry. "The grunters and squeakers don't mind bruised apples."

The children spent nearly all day in the shady orchard, until Uncle Daniel said Bert and Harry had done enough work for the time.

"Then let's get our poles and go fishing," suggested Harry.

They did go, but got no bites. Harry said that morning was the best time to fish.

When Flossie and Freddie became tired of picking apples up from the ground, they found an old swing, and took turns in this, having lots of fun.

Snoop and Snap enjoyed their life in the country. Snoop did not go far from the house. There was another cat there, and the two soon became great friends. Snap also found other dogs with whom he could romp and play in the long meadow grass.

Mrs. Bobbsey and Aunt Sarah spent many hours talking over matters of interest to them, while Dinah, and Martha, who was Aunt Sarah's cook, spent most of their time in the kitchen, making good things to eat.

"'Cause dem chilluns suttinly does eat a turrible lot!" exclaimed Dinah, as she finished making several pies.

Picking the apples kept Uncle Daniel and his men busy for a number of days. Harry had to help, for everyone on a farm has to work, and Bert always lent his cousin a hand. But there were times when they were allowed a play-spell. Sometimes Tom Mason, another country boy, would come over, and, when the work was done, the three boys would go off to have good times together.

One or two days it rained, and then nothing could be done out of doors in the way of farm work. During one of the rainy days Bert and Harry went fishing.

"We'll be sure to get plenty of bites to-day," Harry said, as they started off with their poles and lines, well protected from the weather by rubber boots and coats.

"I hope we catch a lot of fish," said Bert

But they caught only two little sun-fish,

which Harry threw back into the creek, as they were too small to keep.

"I guess we'll have to wait for a sunny day," sighed Harry, as they started home. "I thought rain was good fishing-weather, but it doesn't seem to be."

"Never mind, we had a good time, anyhow," Bert answered.

When the two boys reached the farmhouse, they found Flossie, Freddie, Nan and Mabel Herold sitting in the dining-room, all talking at once, it seemed.

"And we'll take five baskets of lunch," Freddie was saying, "and my fire engine is unpacked now, so I can take that with us, and I'll squirt water on snakes and—and other things."

"Oh, snakes!" cried Mabel. "I hope we don't see any of the horrid things!"

"I'm not afraid!" boasted Freddie.

"Maybe there won't be any," suggested Nan.

"Well, I'm going to take my doll, anyhow," said Flossie.

"What's this all about?" asked Bert. "Are you going somewhere?"

"Picnic!" exclaimed Flossie. "We're going to have a picnic!"

"I'm going!" added Freddie, as though he was afraid of being left.

"We all are," added Nan.

"First I heard about it," Harry said, with a laugh.

"We planned it while you and Bert were off fishing," spoke his mother. "The children are going to take their lunch to the woods in a day or two, as soon as the weather clears."

A few days later the sun came out from behind the clouds, the rain ceased falling and with joyous shouts and laughter the Bobbsey twins, cousin Harry, and some country boys and girls, who had been invited, went off on a woodland picnic.

CHAPTER VIII

LOST IN THE HAY

"OH, isn't it just lovely in the woods," sighed Nan, as she sat down on a green mossy seat beneath a great oak tree. "I could live here forever!"

"So could I!" exclaimed Mabel Herold. "There is no place so lovely as the woods."

"You—you wouldn't stay here all night, would you?" asked Freddie, as he set down the basket of sandwiches he had been carrying, and looked at a dark hole under some bushes.

"I wouldn't mind," sighed Nan again. "It is so lovely here."

"I used to think I liked the seashore best," said Mabel, "but now I think the country is prettiest."

"Well, I'm not going to stay here all night," decided Freddie. "There—there's bugs—and—and—things!"

"I thought you weren't afraid of them," spoke Nan with a smile.

"I--I meant in daytime—I'm not afraid then," declared Freddie. "But at night, why—why, I'd rather be home in bed."

"And I guess we all would," exclaimed Nan, hugging the little fat fellow.

"Oh, there goes a rabbit!" cried Bert to Harry. "Let's see if we can catch him!"

"Come on!" agreed the country boy.

"I'm with you!" shouted Tom Mason.

"Oh, will they hurt the little bunny?" asked Flossie, with quivering lips, for she dearly loved all animals.

"I guess there isn't much danger of them catching the rabbit," said Mr. Bobbsey, sitting down beside his wife in a shady green spot. "A bunny can hop very fast."

And so it proved.. The three boys raced about through the woods until they were quite tired, and very much heated up. But the rabbit got safely away.

"Ah, well, we didn't want him anyhow," said Harry, fanning himself with his cap, after the chase.

"No," agreed Bert, "we just wanted to see if we could get him."

"My! It's warm!" exclaimed Tom, looking at the basket in which the lemonade was packed in bottles. "I'm very thirsty," he said.

"You must not drink when you are too warm," advised Mr. Bobbsey. "Wait until you cool off a bit. If you take cold water, or icy lemonade, into your stomach after you are all heated up from running, you may be made ill. Rest a while before you drink, is good advice."

So the boys waited, and a little later they were allowed to have some of the cool lemonade.

"Are we going to eat our lunch here?" asked Freddie.

"No, a little farther on in the woods,' said his Aunt Sarah.

So they walked on, under the shady trees, with the green carpet of moss under foot, until they came to a little glade, where the trees grew in a circle about a grassy space.

"It—it's just like a circus ring!" exclaimed Freddie. "Oh, couldn't we have a circus, or a show, while we're here at the farm?" he asked.

"We'll see," half-promised his mother.

The table-cloth was spread out on the green grass, and the wooden plates set on it. Then the lunch baskets were opened and the good things passed around. There were sandwiches of several kinds, and cake and cookies, as well as more lemonade.

"Isn't it nice to eat this way?" asked Mrs. Bobbsey. "When we have finished, there are no dishes to wash; just the wooden plates to throw away."

"Yes'm," declared Dinah, with a chuckle. "I spects dish yeah would be a good way to do back home—but it would be kinder cold, eatin' out in de woods in de winter time."

"I wouldn't want to live here in winter," said Freddie. "There isn't any place to hang up your stocking Christmas, and no chimney for Santa Claus to come down!" he added.

"And that would never do!" laughed Mr. Bobbsey. "But we will enjoy these woods all we can."

When the woodland picnic lunch was finished, the party sat about on the grass, in the shade of the trees, and Mr. Bobbsey told stories to the two small children. Flossie and Freddie enjoyed this very much.

Nan and Mabel went for a little walk in the woods, and Bert and Harry said they were going to try for some fish, as they had brought hooks and lines along, and could cut poles in the woods. This time they had very good luck.

"I have one!" suddenly called Harry, pulling up his line. There was a flash, as of silver, in the air, and he hauled a fish up from the water, landing it flapping on the grass behind him.

"Oh, what a big one!" cried Bert, running over to look. "I wish I could get one now."

"Maybe you will," said Harry, trying to catch the flopping creature. "Put on some fresh bait." But Harry caught another fish before Bert had even a good bite.

By this time Mr. Bobbsey had finished his story, and Flossie had taken out her doll to pretend to get it to sleep. Freddie wandered over to where Bert and Harry were fishing.

"Oh, I have one! I have one!" Bert suddenly shouted, and he, too, landed a good-sized fish. It was taken off the hook, and strung on a willow twig, and then, fastened so it could not swim away, it was put back into the water to keep fresh until it was time to go home.

Freddie was very much interested in the captive fish. He went down to the edge of the creek to watch them as they tried to swim away. But they could not, for the willow twigs held them.

Suddenly one of the fish gave a big jump in the shallow pool, where Bert had put them.

"Oh!" exclaimed Freddie, springing back. Then his foot slipped on a wet, mossy stone, and the next moment the little fellow fell down into the water.

"Bert!! Harry! Come and get me! I'm in!" he cried.

Bert and Harry dropped their poles and came up on the run, but there was no danger, for the water was only a few inches deep, near shore, and Freddie was already on his feet when they reached him.

"Oh! Oh!" sobbed the little fellow. "I—I'm all wet."

"Never mind, you have your old clothes on," said his brother. "And I'll tell mother it was an accident."

It was a warm summer day and a little wetting would not harm Freddie. He was taken back to a sunny place by Bert, and told to sit in the warm spot until he had dried out. Then the two larger boys went back to fish, but Freddie's accident must have scared all the fish away, for Bert and Harry caught no more.

"My, but you are a sight, Freddie!" exclaimed Mrs. Bobbsey, when she saw the wet and muddy little twin. "But I suppose you could not help it."

"No, mamma," he answered. "The fish made me fall in."

It was almost time for the picnic party to start back home now. Dinah was packing up the knives, forks, and glasses, and throwing away the wooden plates.

As she knelt over to fold up the table-cloth, she felt something touch her back, and the next moment something cold and wet touched her cheek.

"Go 'long wif yo' now, Bert!" she exclaimed, not turning around. "Don't yo' put any ob dem wet slimy fish on me. Don't you do it!"

Then something almost pushed Dinah over, and again she felt the wet object on the back of her neck.

"Stop it! Stop it!" cried the colored cook. "Don't yo' put any toad down mah back, Bert!"

"I'm not doing anything," Bert answered, and at the sound of his voice Dinah looked up and saw him some distance off. At the same time, though, Bert and Harry burst into a laugh.

"Oh, look what Dinah thought was me!" cried Bert.

Dinah turned around, just as a loud "Moo!" sounded in her ear, making her jump.

"Good land ob massy!" she cried. "It's a cow!"

And, surely enough, so it was. The cow had

wandered out of the woods, and, coming up behind Dinah, had licked her neck with a big red tongue. Perhaps the cow thought Dinah was a lump of black salt!

"Go 'way! Go 'long outer heah! Leef me be!" screamed Dinah, and catching up a handful of wooden plates she threw them at the cow. They rattled on the animal's horns, and then, with another "Moo!" the creature turned and crashed back through the bushes.

"And Dinah thought that was I, tickling her with a fish tail," said Bert, laughing.

"Dat's what I did, honey!" the colored cook said, with a laugh. "I s'pected yo' was up to some ob yo' all tricks!"

They all laughed at this, and amid much fun and jollity the picnic things were packed up and the homeward walk begun.

"Oh, we have had *such* a good time!" sighed Nan. "I am sorry it is over."

"Oh, we'll have more good times," said Bert, as he and Harry walked along with the fish they had caught. Their chum, Tom Mason, had two smaller ones.

There were days of work and play on the

farm, and Harry had his share of tasks to perform. Bert helped him all he could. One day, when the boys and girls had counted on going out rowing on a little lake not far from Meadow Brook, it rained. When they arose in the morning, ready for their fun, the big drops were splashing down.

"Oh, we can't go!" sighed Freddie. "I don't like rain!"

"I thought all firemen liked water," his father said, with a laugh.

"This is too much water!" went on the little chap. "We can't have any fun."

"Oh, yes, we can," said Harry. "We can go out in the barn and play in the hay. The big barn is full of new hay now, and we can slide down the mow and play hide and go seek in it."

"That will be great!" exclaimed Bert. "Come on."

Snap, the dog, must have thought he was also invited, for ne ran out barking, with the children. Umbrellas kept the rain off them until they reached the barn, and then began a good time.

They went to the top of the big pile of fragrant hay in the mow, and slid down it to the barn floor, where a carpet of more hay made a soft place on which to fall. Snap slid with the rest, barking and wagging his tail every minute.

"Now let's play hide and go seek!" suggested Harry after a bit. "I'll 'blind' and when I say 'ready or not, I'm coming,' I'm going to start to find you."

The game began. Harry closed his eyes, so he would not see where the others hid, and Nan, Bert and the rest of them picked out spots in the hay, and about the barn where they thought Harry could not see them. But Harry knew the old barn well, and he easily found Bert. Then he spied Nan and Flossie, hiding together. A little later he discovered where Tom Mason and Mabel Herold were.

"Now I've only to find Freddie," said the country cousin. But Freddie was not so easy to find. Harry looked all over but could not locate him.

"There are so many holes in the barn," the country boy said, "and Freddie is so small, that I guess I'd better give him up. I'll let him come in free. Givey-up! Givey-up!" he called. "Come on in free, Freddie."

But Freddie did not answer. They all kept quiet, but all they could hear was the patter of rain drops on the barn roof.

"Freddie! Freddie! Freddie! Where are you?" cried Nan.

"Come on in free!" added Harry.

"Come on, little fat fireman," went on Bert. "Harry won't tag you, and you can hide again."

But Freddie's childish voice did not reply. The boys and girls looked anxiously at one another.

"Where's Freddie?" asked Flossie, and her lips began to tremble as they did just before she started to cry.

"Oh, we'll find him," said Bert, easily.

"Yes, he's probably hiding so far off he can't hear us," went on Harry.

"Maybe he's lost under the hay," suggested Tom. "I read of a boy getting caught under a pile of hay once, and they didn't get him out for a long time."

"Oh, Freddie's lost! Freddie's lost!" cried Flossie, bursting into tears.

CHAPTER IX

THE FIVE-PIN SHOW

"HUSH, Flossie, don't cry, dear!" begged Nan, putting her arms around her little sister.

"But—but I—I can't help it," stammered Flossie. "Freddie's losted!"

"We'll find him!" said Bert. "He's somewhere inside the barn, that is sure. He'd never go out in all this rain," for the big drops were now coming down thick and fast.

"Freddie isn't afraid of water—he's a fireman—papa's little fat fireman, and I'm papa's little fat fairy, and Freddie's losted—and—and—oh, dear!" sobbed Flossie, as she thought of her missing brother.

"Come on, let's start in all together and find him," suggested Harry. "He must be hid somewhere around here."

"Away down under the hay," suggested Tom Mason.

"Hush! Don't say that," spoke Bert in a low tone. "You'll scare the girls!"

"Maybe we'd better go tell papa and mamma," said Nan.

"Let's try by ourselves, first," suggested her brother. "We'll find Freddie, never fear."

The children began a search of the barn, now almost filled with sweet-smelling hay. Up and down in the mow they looked to find where Freddie might have hidden himself away. They called and shouted to him, but no answer came.

"I don't see why he doesn't reply to us," said Nan to Bert. "He wouldn't keep quiet when we've told him he could come in free. Freddie is too fond of playing hide and go seek to stay away, unless he had to. I am afraid something has happened to him, Bert."

"What could happen to him?" he asked.

"Oh, I don't know, but——" and Nan hesitated and looked worried.

Where could Freddie have hidden himself away in the hay, and stranger, still, why did he not answer the many calls made for him? For the children kept shouting as they searched.

Bert had made up his mind, after looking about for some time, that perhaps, after all, he had better go into the house and tell his father what had happened. Just then Tom Mason slid down from a high part of the haymow to a little hollowed-out place. As he landed, a crackling sound was heard, and then Tom cried:

"Oh, my! Now I have done it! Oh, dear! What a mess! Oh! Oh!"

"Have you found him? Is Freddie there?" asked Flossie from where she stood in the middle of the barn floor.

"No, but I slid right into a hen's nest, and I've broken all the eggs!" cried Tom. "Oh, me! Oh, my!"

He managed to get to his feet, and there he stood, his hands held out in front of him, for they were dripping with the whites and yolks of the broken eggs. Tom's clothes were pretty well splashed up.

"What a sight I am!" he murmured. "And I've broken all the eggs!"

"Never mind! You couldn't help it," said Harry kindly. "The old hen oughtn't to have laid her eggs in here, and they wouldn't have been smashed. Hens like to steal away, and lay their eggs in hay."

"Oh, but you do look *so* funny!" cried Nan, and she laughed in spite of her worry about lost Freddie.

"He—he looks like a cake before it's baked!" giggled Mabel.

They all laughed heartily at Tom's sorry plight.

"Please lend me a handkerchief, somebody," he begged. "I can't reach in my pocket to get mine, and there's some egg running in my eye."

"I'll wipe it for you," offered Bert, laughing so heartily that he could hardly stand up.

"Hark! What's that?" suddenly asked Nan.

They all stopped laughing at once. From somewhere down in the hay, near the smashed nest of eggs, came a voice, asking:

"What's the matter? Isn't anybody going to find me?"

"It's Freddie!" cried Nan.

"Freddie!" shouted Bert. "Where are you?"

"Oh, Freddie is found! Freddie isn't lost any more!" exclaimed Flossie, jumping up and down in delight.

And then, from a little nest in the hay, crawled Freddie himself, rubbing his eyes, and pulling wisps from his tousled hair.

"Have you been there all the while?" asked Harry.

"I—I guess so," answered Freddie, as if he hardly knew himself.

"Well, then, why didn't you answer us?" asked Nan. "We were so frightened about you, Freddie. Why didn't you answer when we called?"

"I—I guess I was asleep," he said. "I didn't hear you until you all began to laugh. Then I woke up."

And that was what had happened. Freddie had found a good hiding place in a hole in the hay, and, while waiting for Harry to come and look for him, the little chap had dozed off, it was so warm and cozy in his hay-nest. And he had slept all through the search made for him, not hearing the calls. But when Tom rolled into the hen's nest, and the others laughed so heartily at him, that awakened the sleeping "little fat fireman."

"My! But you gave us a fright!" said Nan. "But it's all right now, dear," and she helped Freddie pull the hay out of his hair.

"I guess we've had enough of this game," suggested Harry. "Let's do something else."

"I'm hungry," announced Freddie. "Can't we play an eating game?"

"I think so," said Bert. "Dinah and Martha were starting to bake cookies before we came out to the barn, and they ought to be done now. Let's go in."

Into the house, through the rain, tramped the children, and soon, eating cookies, they were telling about Freddie going to sleep in the hay, and Tom trying to make an omelet of himself in the hen's nest.

"Well, this certainly was a nice day, even if it did rain," said Nan, as they were ready to go to bed that night. "I wonder what we can do to-morrow?"

"I know," answered Bert. "Harry and I have a fine plan."

"Oh, tell me what it is," begged his sister.

"It's a secret," he laughed as he went upstairs.

After breakfast next morning Nan, who did not get up very early, looked for Harry and her brother.

"Where are the boys?" she asked her mother.

"Out in the barn," was the answer. "They took some big sheets of paper with them."

"They must be going to make kites," Nan said.

But when she saw what Bert and Harry were doing, she knew it was not a kite game they were planning. For in letters, made with a black stick on the sheets of paper, Nan read the words:

FIVE-PIN SHOW

COME ONE COME ALL

"Oh, what is it?" she cried. "Please tell me, Bert!"

"We're going to have a show," said Harry, "and we're going to charge five pins to come in."

"Oh, may I be in it?" asked Nan. "I'll do anything you want me to. Mayn't I be in it?"

"Shall we let her?" asked Bert of his country cousin.

"Sure," said Harry kindly. "We boys won't be enough. We'll have to have the girls."

"Where's it going to be?" asked Nan.

"Here in the barn," her brother said. "We're going to make a cage for Snap—he's going to be the lion."

"Can Snoop be one of the animals, too?" she inquired.

"Yes, Snoop will be the black tiger," decided Harry. "I only hope he keeps awake, and growls now and then. That will make it seem real."

"Snoop sometimes growls when he gets a piece of meat," suggested Nan.

"Then we'll give him meat in the show," decided Bert.

He and Harry finished making the show bills, and then began to get ready for the performance. With some old sheets they made a curtain across one corner of the barn, in front of the haymow. Nan helped with this, as she could use a needle, thread and thimble better than could the boys.

Then Tom Mason, Mabel Herold and some other of the country boys and girls came over, and they were allowed to be in the show. Bert was to be a clown, and he put on an old suit, turned inside out, and whitened his face with starch, which he begged from Martha.

Harry was to be the wild animal trainer, and show off the black tiger, which was Snoop, and the fierce lion in a cage, which lion was only Snap, the dog.

The show was not to take place until the next day, as Bert said the performers needed time for practice. But some of the "show bills" were fastened up about the village streets, and many boys and girls said they would come if they could get the five pins.

Finally all was ready for the little play. Flossie was made door-keeper and took up the admission pins. Freddie wanted to be a fireman in the show, so they let him do this. His mother made a little red coat for him, and he had his toy fire engine that pumped real water.

"But you mustn't squirt it on anyone in the audience," cautioned Bert.

"No, I'll just squirt it on the wild animals if they get bad," said the little fellow.

Nan was to be a bare-back rider, and Harry had made her a wooden steed from a saw-horse, with rope for reins. Nan perched herself up on the saw-horse, and pretended she was galloping about the ring.

A number of boys and girls came to the show, each one bringing the five pins, so that Flossie had many of them to stick on the cushion which was her cash-box.

Bert was very funny as a clown, and he turned somersaults in the hay. Once he landed on a hard place on the barn floor, and cried:

"Ouch!"

Everyone laughed at that, and they laughed harder when Bert made a funny face as he rubbed his sore elbow.

Harry exhibited Snoop and Snap as the wild animals, but Snoop rather spoiled the performance by not growling as a black tiger should.

"This tiger used to be very wild, ladies and gentlemen," said Harry, "and no keeper dared go in the cage with him. But he is a good tiger now, and loves his keeper," and Harry put his hand in, and stroked Snoop, who purred happily.

"Oh, I think this is a lovely show!" exclaimed Nellie Johnson. "I'm coming every day."

A little later, near the box which had been made into a cage for Snoop, there came a loud noise. Snoop meowed very hard, and hissed as he used to do when he saw a strange dog. At the same time something went:

"Gobble-obbleobble!" Then came a great crash, more cries from Snoop and out into the middle of the barn floor dashed the black cat with a big, long-legged, feathered creature clinging to poor Snoop's tail.

"Oh! Oh! Oh!" cried Flossie. "The wild animals are loose!"

CHAPTER X

A SHAM BATTLE

FOR a few moments there was wild confusion in that part of the barn where the "show" was going on. Nan gave one look at the strange mixture of the howling Snoop and the gobbling bird in the centre of the floor, and then, catching Flossie up in her arms, Nan made a spring for the haymow.

"Wait! Wait!" cried Flossie. "I'm losing all the pins! I've dropped the pin cushion!"

That was her cash-box—the pins she had taken in as admission to the little play.

"We can't stop for it now!" cried Nan. "We must get out of the way."

"The cat has a fit!" cried Tom Mason.

"Oh, poor Snoop!" wailed Flossie.

"Grab him, somebody!" shouted Harry.

"No, let Snoop alone!" advised Bert. "He

might bite, if you touched him now, though he wouldn't mean to."

"But what is it? What gave him the fit?" asked Mabel Herold.

"Our old turkey gobbler," answered Harry. "The gobbler has caught Snoop by the tail. It's enough to give any cat a fit."

"I should say so!" cried Bert. "Look out! They're coming over this way! Look out!"

The children scrambled to one side, for Snoop and the big turkey gobbler were sliding, rolling and tumbling over the barn floor toward the board seats where the show audience, but a little while before, were enjoying the performance.

The girls had followed Nan and Flossie up to a low part of the haymow, and were out of the way. But the boys wanted to be nearer where they could see what was going on.

The noise and the excitement had roused Snap, the dog, who had curled up in his cage and was sleeping, after having been exhibited as a raging and roaring lion, and now Snap was barking and growling, trying to understand what was going on. Perhaps he wanted to join in the fun, for it was fun for the turkey gobbler, if it was not for poor Snoop.

"Look out the way! Clear the track! Toot! Toot!" came a sudden cry and little Freddie came running toward the gobbler and cat, dragging after him his much-prized toy fire engine.

"Get back out of the way, Freddie!" ordered Bert. "Snoop may scratch or bite you, or the gobbler may pick you. Get out of the way!"

"I'm a fireman!" cried the fat little fellow. "Firemans never get out of the way! Toot! Toot! Clear the track! Chuu! Chuu! Chuu!" and he puffed out his cheeks, making a noise like an engine.

"You must come here!" insisted Bert, making a spring toward his little brother.

"I can't come back! Firemans never come back!" half screamed Freddie. "I'm going to squirt water on the bad gobble-obble bird that's biting my Snoop!"

And then, before anyone could stop him, Freddie unreeled the little rubber hose of his fire engine, and pointed the nozzle at the struggling gobbler and cat in the middle of the barn floor.

I have told you, I think, that Freddie's engine held real water, and, by winding up a spring a little pump could be started, squirting a stream of water for some distance.

"Whoop! Here comes the water!" cried Freddie, as he started the pump working.

Then a stream shot out, right toward the cat and turkey. It was the best plan that could have been tried for separating them.

With a howl and a yowl Snoop pulled his claws loose from where they were tangled up in the turkey's feathers. With a final gobble, the turkey let go of Snoop's tail. The water spurted out in a spraying stream, Freddie's engine being a strong one, for a toy.

"That's the way I do it!" cried Freddie, just like Mr. Punch. "That's the way I do it! Look, I made them stop!"

"Why—why, I believe you did!" exclaimed Bert, with a laugh.

The gobbler ran out through the open barn door, his feathers wet and bedraggled. He must have thought he had been caught in a rainstorm. And poor Snoop was glad enough to crawl away in a dark corner, to lick himself dry with his red tongue.

"Poor Snoop!" said Freddie, as he stopped his engine from pumping any more water. "I'm sorry I got you wet, Snoop, but I couldn't help it. I only meant to sprinkle the gobbler"

He patted Snoop, who began purring.

"Well, I guess that ends the show," said Bert, who looked funnier than ever now, as a clown, for the white on his face was streaked in many ways with the water, some of which had sprayed on him.

"Yes, the performance is over," announced Harry.

"Oh, but it was lovely!" said Nan, as she slid down the hay with Flossie. "I don't see how you boys ever got it up."

"Oh, we're smart boys!" laughed Harry.

"But I lost all the pins!" wailed Flossie. "Nan wouldn't let me stop to pick them up!"

"I should say not! With that queer wild animal bursting in on us!" exclaimed Mabel. "Oh, but I was so frightened!"

"Pooh! I wasn't!" boasted Freddie. "I

knew my fire engine would scare them."

"Well, it did all right," announced Bert. "I guess we'd better let Snap out now," he said, for the dog was barking loudly, and trying to break out of the packing box of which his cage was made.

Snoop's cage was broken, where the black cat had forced his way out.

"His tail must have been hanging down through the bars," explained Bert, "and the gobbler came along and nipped it. That made Snoop mad, and he got out and clawed the turkey."

"I guess that was it," agreed Harry. "Well, we had fun anyhow, if Snoop and the turkey did have a hard time."

Snoop was soon dry again, and not much the worse for what had happened to him. The gobbler, except for the loss of a few feathers, was not hurt. But after that the turkey and cat kept well out of each other's way.

Everyone voted the show a great success, and the children planned to have another one before they left Meadow Brook farm. But the Bobbsey twins did not know all that was in store for them before they went back to the city.

One day, when they were all seated at dinner in the pleasant Bobbsey farmhouse, Uncle Daniel paused, with a piece of pie half raised on his fork, and said:

"Hark!"

"What's the matter?" asked Aunt Sarah. "Did you think you heard the old ram coming again?"

"No, but it sounded like thunder," replied her husband, "and if it's going to rain I must hurry, and get those tomatoes picked."

"I heard something, too," said Mr. Bobbsey.

"So did I," spoke up Freddie. "Maybe it's the old black bull down in the pasture."

"No. There it goes again!" said Uncle Daniel. "It must be thunder!"

There sounded a dull distant booming noise, that was repeated several times.

Uncle Daniel got up hastily from the table and went to the door.

"Not a cloud in the sky," he remarked, "and yet that noise is growing louder."

It was, indeed, as they all could hear.

"It's guns, that's what it is," declared Bert. "It sounds like Fourth of July."

"That's what it does," agreed his cousin

Harry. "It's back of those hills. I'm going to see what it is."

"So am I!" cried Bert. The boys had finished their dinners, and now started off on a run in the direction of the booming sounds.

"Come along," said Uncle Daniel to Mr. Bobbsey. "We may as well go also."

"I want to come!" cried Freddie.

"Not now," said his mother. "Wait until papa comes back."

Mr. Bobbsey, with his brother and the two boys, soon reached the top of the hill. All the while the sound like thunder was growing louder Then puffs of smoke could be seen rising in the air.

"What can it be?" asked Bert.

"I can't imagine," answered Harry.

They saw, in another minute, what it was.

Down in a valley below them was a crowd of soldiers, with cannon and guns, firing at one another. The soldiers were divided into two parties. First one party would run forward, and then the other, both sides firing as fast as they could.

"It's a war!" cried Bert. "It's a battle!"

"It's only a sham battle!" said Mr. Bobbsey. "No one is being hurt, for they are using blank cartridges. It must be that the soldiers are practicing so as to know how to fight if a real war comes. It is only a sham battle."

The cannons roared, the rifles rattled and flashes of fire and puffs of smoke were on all sides.

"Oh, look at the horses—the cavalry!" cried Harry, as a company of men, mounted on horses, galloped toward some of the soldiers, who turned their rifles on them.

Then one man, on a big black horse, left the main body and came straight on toward Mr. Bobbsey, Uncle Daniel, and the two boys.

"We'd better look out!" cried Bert. "Maybe he wants to capture us!"

CHAPTER XI

MOVING PICTURES

THE man on the black horse continued to ride toward the two boys, Uncle Daniel and Mr. Bobbsey. Behind him more men on horses rushed forward, but they were going toward some soldiers on foot, who were firing their rifles at the "cavalry," as Harry called them, that being the name for horse-soldiers.

"Oh, look, some of the men are falling off their horses!" cried Bert.

"Maybe they are hurt," Harry said.

"No, I guess it's only making believe, if this is a sham battle," went on Bert.

By this time the man on the black horse was near Mr. Bobbsey.

"You had better stand farther back, if you don't mind," he said.

"Why, are we in danger here?" asked Uncle Daniel.

"Well, not exactly danger, for we are using only blank cartridges. But you are too near the camera. You'll have your pictures taken if you don't look out," and he smiled, while his horse pawed the ground, making the soldier's sword rattle against his spurs.

"Camera!" exclaimed Mr. Bobbsey. "Is someone taking pictures of this sham battle?"

"Yes, we are taking moving pictures," replied the soldier. "The man with the camera is right over there," and he pointed to a little hill, on top of which stood a man with what looked like a little box on three legs. The man was turning a crank.

"Moving pictures!" repeated Uncle Daniel, looking in the direction indicated.

"That's what this sham battle is for," went on the soldier who sat astride the black horse. "We are pretending to have a hard battle, to make an exciting picture. Soon the camera will be pointed over this way, and as it wouldn't look well to have you gentlemen and boys in the picture, I'll be obliged to you if you'll move back a little."

"Of course we will," agreed Mr. Bobbsey.

"Especially as it looks as though the soldiers were coming our way."

"Yes, part of the sham battle will soon take place here," the cavalryman went on.

"Come on back, boys!" cried Uncle Daniel. "We can watch just as well behind those trees, and we won't be in the way, and have our pictures taken without knowing it."

"Yes, and we won't be in any danger of having some of the paper wadding from a blank cartridge blown into our eyes," added Mr. Bobbsey.

"Say, this is great!" cried Harry. "I'm glad we came."

"So am I," said Bert.

The boys looked on eagerly while the battle kept up. They saw the soldiers charge back and forth. The cannon shot out puffs of white smoke, but no cannon balls, of course, for no one wanted to be hurt. Back and forth rushed the soldiers on horses, and others on foot, firing with their rifles.

Of course they were not real soldiers, but were dressed in soldiers' uniforms to make the picture seem real. I suppose you have often seen in moving picture theatres pictures of a battle.

It was well that Mr. Bobbsey and the others had gotten out of the way, for shortly afterward the men rushed right across the spot where Bert and Harry had been standing.

"If we were there, then we'd have been walked on," said Bert.

"Yes, and we'd have had our pictures taken, too," said Harry, pointing to the man with the camera who had taken a new position.

"I wouldn't mind that, would you?" asked Bert.

"No, I don't know as I would," replied the country cousin. "It would be fun to see yourself in moving pictures, I think. Oh, look! That horse went down, and the soldier shot right over his head."

A horse had stumbled and fallen, bringing down the rider with him. But whether this was an accident, or whether it was done on purpose, to make the moving picture look more natural, the boys could not tell.

The firing was now louder than ever. A number of cannon were being used, horses drawing them up with loud rumblings, while the men wheeled the guns into place, loaded and fired them.

On all sides men were falling down, pretending to be shot, for those who took the moving pictures wanted them to seem as nearly like real war as possible.

"Oh, here they are!" suddenly exclaimed a voice back of Mr. Bobbsey and the others.

Turning, Bert saw his mother, with Aunt Sarah, Flossie, Freddie and Nan. They had come up the hill to look down into the valley and see what all the excitement was about.

"Yes, here we are!" cried Mr. Bobbsey. "Isn't this great? It's a sham battle."

"What for?" asked his wife, and she had to speak loudly to be heard above the rattle and bang of the guns.

"For moving pictures," answered Mr. Bobbsey, pointing to the men with the cameras, for now three or four of them were at work, taking views of the "fight" from different places.

"Mercy! What a racket!" exclaimed Aunt Sarah.

"Oh, I don't like it!" cried Flossie, covering her ears with her chubby hands. "Take me away, mamma; I'm afraid of the guns!"

"Pooh! There's nothing to be scared of!" exclaimed Freddie. "I'm going to be a soldier when I grow up, and shoot a gun."

"You can't play with me if you do," declared Flossie, when the bang of the cannon stopped for a moment, leaving the air quiet.

"I don't want to play with girls—I'm going to be a fighting soldier!" declared Freddie. "Hi! Hark to the guns! Boom! Boom!" and he jumped up and down as the cannon thundered again.

"Oh, I don't like it! I want to go home and play with my doll!" half-sobbed Flossie. "I don't like fighting."

"And I don't, either," said Nan, though she was not afraid. It was the noise for which she did not care.

"Hi! That was a fine one!" cried Freddie, as one of the largest cannon fired a blank shot at a group of horse soldiers.

"Please take me home!" sobbed Flossie, and there were tears in her blue eyes now.

"Yes, we'll go home," said Mrs. Bobbsey.

"You can play you are a nurse, Flossie, and take care of your doll. We'll leave the battle to the boys and men."

"I can stay, can't I?" asked Freddie, who was delighted at the lively scene down below, and he jumped about in delight as cannon after cannon went off.

"Yes, you may stay," said his father. "We'll look after him," he added to his wife.

Freddie crowded up to where Bert and Harry were eagerly watching the sham battle, and stood between his brother and cousin.

"Boom! Boom!" he cried. "I like this!"

But little Flossie covered her ears with her hands and went on down the hill, toward the farmhouse, with her mother and aunt. Nan went with them also, as she said the firing made her head ache.

CHAPTER XII

THE BOBBSEYS ACT

"WELL, I guess the battle is over now," said Bert, after a while. The cannon had stopped firing, and the "soldiers" no longer "shot" at each other with their rifles.

"See, the men on horses have captured the other men," spoke Harry. And he pointed to where the cavalry had surrounded a number of the foot soldiers, or infantry, as they are called, and were driving them over the fields toward some log cabins.

"They must have built those log houses on purposes for the moving picture play," said Uncle Daniel. "For they weren't here the other day, when I was over in this valley."

"Very likely they did," agreed Mr. Bobbsey. "It takes a great deal of work to make a moving picture play now-a-days, and often a company will build a whole house, only to set fire to it, or tear it down to make a good picture."

"If they set a house on fire," broke in Freddie, "I could put it out with my fire engine, and I'd be in the movies then."

"Oh, you and your fire engine!" laughed Bert, ruffling up his little brother's hair. "You think you can do anything with it."

"Well, I stopped the turkey gobbler from eating up Snoop," Freddie cried. "Didn't I?"

"So you did!" exclaimed Harry. "You and your fire engine are all right, Freddie."

The soldiers who had fallen off their horses, or who had toppled over in the grass, to pretend that they were shot in battle, now got up—"coming to life," Bert called it.

The battle scene was over, but the men were not yet done using the cameras, for they took them farther down the valley toward the log cabins. The soldiers were now grouped around these buildings, and Bert and Harry could see several ladies, in brightly colored dresses, mingled with the soldiers in uniform.

"I wonder what they are doing now?" asked Bert.

"Oh, taking a more peaceful scene for the

movies," answered his father. "They have had enough of war, I guess."

"That would suit Flossie," remarked Uncle Daniel with a laugh.

The valley was now quiet, but over it hung a cloud of smoke from the cannon. The wind was, however, blowing the smoke away.

"Can we go up to the log cabins and watch them make more pictures, father?" asked Bert

"Well, yes, I guess so; if you don't get in the way of the cameras. Do you want to come?" asked Mr. Bobbsey of Uncle Daniel. "You don't often get a chance to see moving pictures out here, I guess. Better come."

"No, not now, thank you," was the answer "I must get back and look after my tomatoes. They need to be picked. But you can go on with the boys."

So Mr. Bobbsey took Bert and Harry up to where other moving pictures were being made. The boys did not understand all that was being done, but they watched eagerly just the same.

They saw men and soldiers talking to the ladies, who were members of the moving picture company. Then they saw soldiers who pretended to have been hurt in the sham-battle, being put on cots, and bandaged up.

"This is a make-believe hospital," Mr. Bobbsey explained to the boys. "They want it to look as natural as possible, you see."

The boys watched while "doctors" went among the "wounded," giving them "medicine," all make-believe, of course. Then one of the ladies, dressed as a nurse, came through the rows of cots which were placed in the open air, under some trees.

"How do you like it?" asked one of the moving picture men of Mr. Bobbsey, coming over to where Bert's father was standing. The man had been turning the crank of one of the cameras, but, just then, he had nothing to do.

"It is very interesting," said Mr. Bobbsey. "We heard your firing and came over to look on. Are you going to be here long?"

"Only a few days. But there will be no more battle pictures. They cost too much money to make. The rest of the scenes will be more peaceful."

"That would suit my little girl," said Mr. Bobbsey, with a laugh. "She didn't like the cannon and guns."

"Oh, have you a little girl?" asked the moving picture man, who seemed to be one of those in charge of the actors and actresses.

"Yes, I have a little girl," Mr. Bobbsey replied.

"And these two boys?" asked the camera man.

"No, only one of the boys is mine," and Bert's father nodded at his son. "The other is my nephew."

"Do you live around here?" the man went on. "Excuse my asking you so many questions," he continued. "My name is Weston, and I have charge of making these moving pictures. We need some children to take small parts in one of the scenes, and, as we have no little ones in our company, I was wondering whether we could not get some country boys and girls to pose for us, or, rather, act for us, for we want them to move, not to just stand still. And I thought if you lived around here," he said to Mr. Bobbsey, "you might know where we could borrow a dozen children for an hour or so."

"I don't live here," Mr. Bobbsey replied, "but I am staying on my brother's farm. What sort of acting do you want the children to do for the moving pictures?"

"Oh, something very simple. You see, one of the ladies in our company is supposed to be a school teacher before the war breaks out. We have taken the war scenes already--that sham battle you looked at was all we need of that.

"The school teacher goes to the front as a nurse, but before she goes, we want a scene showing her in front of the school surrounded by her pupils."

"I see," said Mr. Bobbsey.

"Now we have the schoolhouse," said Mr. Weston, "or, rather, there is an old schoolhouse down the road that will do very nicely to photograph. We have permission to use it, as this is vacation time. We also have the lady who will act as the teacher, and, later as the Red Cross nurse. But we need children to act as school pupils.

"I thought perhaps you might know of some children who would like to act for the movies," the man went on. "It will take only a little time, and it will not be at all unpleasant.

They will just have to act naturally, as any school children would do."

"Well, I have four children of my own," said Mr. Bobbsey, as he thought of his two sets of twins, "and my brother has a boy. There are also several children in the village. Perhaps it could be arranged to have their pictures taken."

"I hope it can!" exclaimed Mr. Weston. "I'll talk to you about it in a few minutes. I must go see about this hospital scene now."

He hurried away, while Bert and Harry looked at one another

"Do you want to be in the movies?" asked Mr. Bobbsey.

"I don't mind," spoke Harry, smiling.

"Neither do I," added Bert. "Freddie would like it, too, but Flossie wouldn't come if they shot any guns."

"They wouldn't shoot guns where children were," said Mr. Bobbsey. "I'll see what your mother, and Uncle Daniel and Aunt Sarah say."

Later that day the moving picture man explained just what was wanted, and as Mrs.

Bobbsey and Aunt Sarah had no objections, it was decided to let the Bobbsey twins, as well as Harry, take part in the moving pictures. Tom Mason, Mabel Herold and some others of the country village were also to be in the scene.

It was taken, or "filmed," as the moving picture people say, the next morning. Down to the old schoolhouse, on the country road, went the children, laughing and talking, a little bit shy, some of them.

But the actress who was to pretend to be a school teacher was so nice that she soon made the little children feel at ease. Flossie and Freddie loved her from the first, and each insisted upon walking along with her, hand in hand.

"That will make a pretty picture," said the moving picture man. "Just walk along the road, Miss Burns," he said to the actress, "with Flossie on one side, and Freddie on the other. I'll take your pictures as if you were going to school."

This was done. Flossie and Freddie soon forgot that they were really "acting" for the movies, and were as natural as could be wished.

"I—I've got a fire engine!" said Freddie, as he trudged along with the actress-teacher.

"Have you, indeed?" she asked pleasantly. "Don't look at the camera," she cautioned Flossie. "Just pretend it isn't there."

"And I've got a doll!" Flossie said, not to let Freddie get the best of her.

"And my fire engine pumps real water," Freddie went on, "and I squirted it on our cat and on the old turkey gobbler."

"Oh, but why did you do that?" asked the actress. "Wasn't that unkind?"

"Oh, no!" exclaimed Freddie, his eyes big and round. "The gobbler was pinching our cat's tail, and Snoop was scratching the turkey. I had to squirt water on them to make them stop."

"Oh, I see!" exclaimed Miss Burns with a jolly laugh.

"Well, anyhow, my doll can open and shut her eyes," said Flossie. "So I don't care!"

"That's enough of that scene," said Mr. Weston. "Now all you children crowd up around the school steps, as if you were going in after the last bell had rung. Pretend you are going into school."

The village children were a little bashful at first, but Bert, Nan and Harry, taking the lead, showed them what to do, and after one trial everything went off well.

The children grouped themselves about the actress-teacher, who clasped her arms about the shoulders of as many as she could reach. It made a pretty scene in front of the old schoolhouse, with the green trees for a background. The use of the school had been allowed the moving picture company for the day.

"Now play about, as if it were recess," directed Mr. Weston, after the first scene had been taken. "Be as natural as you can. And you grown folks please keep back out of the way," he asked, for Mrs. Bobbsey and a number of the fathers and mothers had come to see their children pose for the moving picture camera.

By this time the children had lost their bashfulness, and were acting as naturally as though they really were at school. They played tag and other simple games, while the camera clicked their images on the celluloid film. Miss Burns, as the teacher, took part in some of the girls' games.

"Now I want a larger boy and girl to walk down the road together, the boy carrying the girl's books," said Mr. Weston. "You'll do." he went on to Nan, "and you," to Harry. Soon the two cousins were strolling along, having their pictures taken.

"I want to go with Nan!" cried Freddie "I want my picture taken some more."

"Not now, dear," said Miss Burns, who was not in the scene with Nan and Harry. "Wait a little."

"No, I want to go with Nan now," insisted Freddie, and he broke from the hand of the actress and rushed after his sister.

"Oh, he'll spoil the picture!" cried Bert, solicitously. "Come back, Freddie; that's a good boy!"

But Freddie did not intend to come back.

"Nan, Nan! Wait for me!" begged Freddie.

Nan did not know what to do. She had been told to walk down the road, pretending to talk to Harry, and to take half an apple which he would hand her, in view of the camera.

"That's all right—let the little fellow get into the picture," directed Mr. Weston. "It will make it all the prettier."

So Freddie had his wish, to walk beside his sister. But he had not gone far before he saw, on the edge of a little brook, a bright red flower.

"I'm going to get it!" he cried. "I can hold it in my hand. It will look nice in the picture."

"No, no!" cried Nan. "Stay with me, Freddie."

"Going to get the flower!" he shouted, as he ran on ahead.

And, just as he reached the edge of the brook, his foot slipped, and down he went with a great splash, into the water.

"Oh, Freddie's fallen in! Freddie's fallen in!" cried Nan, rushing forward.

"I'll pull him out!" cried the man grinding away at the crank of the camera.

"No, you stay there and get the moving picture," said Mr. Watson. "It will make a funny scene, and Freddie is in no danger. The water isn't deep! I'll get him out!"

"That's the second time Freddie's fallen in," said Bert, as he ran toward the brook.

"Help me out! Help me out!" sobbed Freddie, splashing about in the water.

CHAPTER XIII

THE CIRCUS

"THERE you are, my little man! Not hurt a bit! Up again! Out again!" and Mr. Weston picked little Freddie out of the brook, and set him on his feet. "All right, aren't you?" asked the moving picture man.

"Ye—yes, I—I guess so," stammered the "little fat fireman," as he looked down at his dripping knickerbockers. "But I—I'm terrible wet! I'm awful wet—ma—mamma!" he stammered.

"Never mind, Freddie," Mrs. Bobbsey answered with a smile. "You'll dry."

"I say!" called one of the men who had been turning the crank of the moving picture camera. "I say, Mr. Weston, I got the picture of the boy falling in the water on this film. I couldn't help it."

"That's all right," said the manager. "It

won't spoil the picture any. It will only make it look more natural."

"And it's natural for Freddie to be wet," said Bert, with a laugh. "He's always playing with that toy fire engine of his, and getting soaked."

"But I didn't have the fire engine this time, Bert," said the chubby little chap. "I—I fell in!"

"You poor little dear!" exclaimed the actress-schoolteacher, putting her arms around him. "It was all my fault, too!"

"No, it was mine," said Freddie, generously. "I don't mind. I like being wet!"

They all laughed at this. Mrs. Bobbsey said Freddie wanted to be polite.

A few more pictures were made of the village children, the Bobbsey twins, with the exception of Freddie, taking part. Freddie was hurried off by his mother to the farmhouse to be put into dry clothes.

Then, with thanks to those who had helped make the scenes, Mr. Weston, Miss Burns and the camera man went back to the village hotel where they were stopping.

"Wasn't it great, Bert!" exclaimed Harry, as he and his cousin strolled over the fields.

"It certainly was," agreed Bert.

"If we could only see the pictures when they are finished," suggested Mabel Herold. "It must be queer to see yourself in the movies."

"I think so, too," said Nan. "I'm going to find out where this play will be shown, in some theatre, and maybe mamma will take us to it."

"I hope she does," Bert said. "It will be fun to see Freddie falling in."

"Poor little fellow!" murmured Nan.

"But he was real brave," Mabel added.

For several days the Bobbsey twins, their cousin and their country friends talked of the moving pictures in which they had had a part. They went again to the valley, where more scenes were being made, but none were as exciting as the sham-battle.

"Aren't they going to shoot any more guns?" asked Freddie, his eyes big and shining with the hope of excitement.

"I guess that's all over," spoke Bert.

"And I'm glad of it," Nan declared.

"So am I," exclaimed Flossie, looking

around as though she would hear a boom from a cannon.

One day Bert and Harry went alone to the place where the moving picture company had erected tents and log cabins in the valley. They found the men packing things up, taking down the tents and knocking apart the wooden cabins.

"Are you all through?" Bert asked Mr. Weston."

"All through, my lad," was the answer. "We are going to another place soon, to get different moving pictures. But we'll be here for a day or two yet, at least some of the camera men will. They have to take pictures of a circus parade."

"Circus parade!" exclaimed Harry. "Is a circus coming here?"

"Well, not exactly here," replied Mr. Weston. "But it is coming to Rosedale—that's the next town—and I am going to have some moving pictures made of it."

"The circus coming to Rosedale!" cried Bert, looking at Harry. The same thought came to both of them.

"Let's go!" exclaimed Harry, eagerly.

"If our folks will let us," added Bert.

"Oh, I guess mine will," spoke the country boy. "Circuses don't come around here very often, and when they do, we generally go. I do hope they'll let you come, Bert."

"It's going to be a large circus," said Mr. Weston. "They have a good collection of wild animals."

"I don't believe they can beat our combination of a wild cat, Snoop, and a crazy turkey gobbler," said Bert to Harry with a laugh, when the two boys were on their way back to the farmhouse.

Passing along a country road Bert saw something that caused him to cry out:

"Look, there it is, Harry!"

"What?"

"The circus! See it!" and Bert pointed to a barn.

"Oh, you mean the circus posters," went on Harry, for Bert had pointed to the bright-colored pictures advertising the performance. There were shown men jumping through paper hoops or hanging from dizzy heights on trapeze bars, ladies riding galloping horses, and all sorts of wild animals, from the long-necked giraffe to the hippopotamus. who appeared to have no neck at all, and from the big elephant to the little monkey.

"Oh, I do hope we can see it!" cried Bert, as he and his cousin stood before the gay pictures.

"I'm going to do my best to go!" declared Harry.

The two boys hurried home, talking on the way of the circus posters they had seen, and wondering if there really would be shown all the wild animals pictured on the side of the barn.

Bert saw his father and mother sitting out in the side yard under a shady tree, and, running up to them he asked:

"Oh, can't we go? We want to so much! Nan, you ask, too!" he cried.

Mr. and Mrs. Bobbsey looked at him rather surprised.

"What's it all about?" asked Mr. Bobbsey, with a smile.

"And what am I to ask?"

"For a circus—wild animals—moving pictures—the parade—an elephant—lions, tigers —everything!" cried Bert, stopping because he ran out of breath.

"Ask for all that?" exclaimed Nan, wonderingly.

"No, Bert means the circus is coming," explained Harry, with a laugh. "The moving picture people are going to get views of the parade. The posters are up on the barns and fences. It's coming to Rosedale, the circus is, and——"

"Oh, do let us go!" broke in Bert.

Mr. and Mrs. Bobbsey looked at one another, questioningly.

"Oh, wouldn't it be just grand!" sighed Nan.

"What is it?" demanded Freddie, toddling up just then. "Is there going to be a fire? Can I squirt with my engine?"

"Always thinking of that, little fat fireman!" laughed his father. "No, it isn't a fire, Freddie."

"It's a circus coming!" cried Bert. "Can't you take us, father?"

"I'm afraid not, son," he said. "I have just

had a letter calling me back to Lakeport on business."

"Oh!" cried Nan and Bert in a chorus.

"Do we have to go back to the city, too?" asked Bert, after a pause.

"No, I am going to let you and mamma stay here," said Mr. Bobbsey, "but I have to go. I'll come back, of course, but not in time to take you to the circus, I'm afraid."

"Mamma can take us," said Freddie.

"Hardly," said Mrs. Bobbsey with a smile "I want papa along when I have four children to take to a circus."

"My father will take us," said Harry. "He always goes to a circus when one comes around here."

"Oh, fine!" cried Bert. "Uncle Daniel will take us! Uncle Daniel will take us!" and he caught Nan around the waist and went dancing over the lawn with her.

"Now may we go, papa?" asked Nan, when Bert let her go.

"Well, I guess so," answered Mr. Bobbsey "Uncle Daniel can look after you as well as I could."

"If Uncle Daniel goes, it will be all right," Mrs. Bobbsey said.

"And will you go, too, mamma?" asked Bert, slipping up to her, and giving her a kiss.

"Oh, yes, I suppose I'll have to help feed the elephant peanuts," she laughed.

"Hurray! Hurrah!" cried Bert, swinging his cap in the air. "We're going to the circus! We're going to the circus!"

The children were delighted with the pleasure in store for them. They talked of little else, and when thy found that Tom Mason and Mabel Herold were also going to the show, they were more than delighted.

"Oh, what fun we'll have!" cried Nan.

"I—I hope none of the wild animals get loose," said Flossie, with rather a serious face.

"Nonsense! Of course they won't!" cried Bert.

"If they do, I—I'll squirt my fire engine on them!" cried Freddie. "Lions and tigers are afraid of water."

"But elephants aren't, are they, mamma?" asked Flossie. "I saw a picture of an elephant squirting water through his nose-trunk just like your fire engine, Freddie. Elephants aren't afraid of water."

"Well, elephants won't hurt you, anyhow," spoke the little fat fellow. "And if a lion or tiger gets loose, I'll play the hose on him, just as I did at The Five-Pin Show."

Mr. Bobbsey was obliged to go back to the city next day, but he said he would return to Meadow Brook as soon as he could.

"And if you see that poor boy, bring him back with you, and we'll take him to the circus with us," said Freddie.

"What poor boy?" asked Mr. Bobbsey.

"You know, the one who had the no-good money, and who ran away when we were out with you in the auto that time, and the two girls in the boat—don't you remember?" asked Freddie, ending somewhat breathlessly, for that was rather a long sentence for him.

"Oh, you mean Frank Kennedy, who worked for Mr. Mason," said the lumber merchant.

"Yes, that's the boy," went on Freddie. "If you see him, tell him to run this way, and we'll take him to the circus with us."

"Poor boy," sighed Mrs. Bobbsey. "I wonder what has become of him?"

"I don't know," answered her husband. "I'll ask Mr. Mason, if I see him. He said Frank was sure to come back. It is a hard life for a boy to lead. Well, take care of yourselves, children, and I'll come back as soon as I can. Have a good time at the circus."

"We will, papa!" chorused the Bobbsey twins.

Uncle Daniel readily promised to take the whole family to the circus. Rosedale, where the show would be held, in the big tents, was not far from Meadow Brook.

"I'll just hitch up the team to the big wagon," said the farmer, "put plenty of soft straw in the bottom, and we'll go over in style. We'll take our lunch with us, and have a good time."

"Is Dinah going?" asked Flossie.

"Yes, I think we'll take her and Martha, too," said Mrs. Bobbsey, but when Flossie went to tell the colored cook the treat in store for her, Dinah cried:

"'Deed an' I ain't gwine t' no circus.

doan't want t' be et up by no ragin' lion who goeth about seekin' what he may devour, laik it says in de Good Book. Dere's enough wild animiles right yeah on dish year farm—wild bulls, wild rams an' turkey gobblers, what pulls cats by dere tails. No, sah! honey lamb—I ain't gwine t' no circus!"

CHAPTER XIV

FREDDIE IS MISSING

FLOSSIE came back from her talk with Dinah, looking very disappointed.

"What is the matter, dear?" asked her mother, noting the sorrowful look on the little girl's face.

"Dinah isn't going to the circus," said Flossie, almost ready to cry, for she was very fond of the faithful and loving colored woman.

"Oh, I guess she'll go with us," said Mrs. Bobbsey. "Why doesn't she want to come?"

"She's afraid of the wild animals," answered Flossie.

"Pooh! I'm not afraid!" boasted Freddie. "You tell her, Flossie, that I'll take my fire engine along an' scare 'em. Wait, I'll tell her myself."

Out Freddie ran to the kitchen, where Dinah was helping Martha with the baking.

"Don't you be afraid, Dinah!" he cried. "I won't let any of the wild animals get you!"

"Bress yo' heart, honey lamb!" exclaimed the colored cook with a laugh that made her shake "like a bowl full of jelly."

"I—I'll scare 'em off with my fire engine," Freddie went on.

"Will yo', honey lamb? So yo' won't let ole black Dinah get hurted, eh? Well, honey, lamb, I'd gib yo' all a hug but mah hands am all flour," and Dinah held them up for Freddie to see.

"Never mind, you can hug me some other time—you can hug me twice to make up for this," said Freddie. "Now you'll come to the circus, won't you?"

"I—I'll see, honey lamb," Dinah half-promised.

Later Mrs. Bobbsey told the colored cook there would be no danger, and when Dinah learned that Uncle Daniel was going, as well as one of his hired men, she made no more objections.

The day of the circus came, bright and sunny. Everyone was up early in the farmhouse, for Uncle Daniel said they wanted to be in time to see the morning parade. Then they would eat their dinner, which they would take with them, as though it were a picnic, and go to the show in the afternoon.

"Oh, I wish papa were here!" sighed Nan, as she and Bert left the breakfast table.

"Why, you're not afraid, are you?" he asked.

"No, only I'd like him to see the show," she said. Nan was always thoughtful for her father.

"Yes, it would be nicer if he could come with us," agreed Bert. And then he forgot all about it, because he and Harry had a discussion as to whether an elephant or a hippopotamus could eat the most hay.

Work on the farm was almost forgotten that circus day. Uncle Daniel and the hired man did what had to be done, and then the horses were hitched to the big wagon, which was filled with straw.

Mrs. Bobbsey and Aunt Sarah were busy dressing Flossie and Freddie. Bert, Harry and Nan could look out for themselves. Dinah and

Martha were busy in the kitchen putting up the lunch.

"Here comes Tom Mason!" called Bert to his cousin, as he saw the country boy, dressed in his best, coming up the walk.

"Oh, I do hope Mabel isn't late," exclaimed Flossie. Mabel and Tom were to go to the circus with Uncle Daniel, as the guests of the Bobbsey twins.

"There she comes—down the road," announced Harry, after greeting Tom. "Here comes Mabel!"

The children gathered out on the lawn to wait for the older folks. Finally everything was in readiness, the wagon, drawn by the prancing horses, rattled up, and into it piled the children, sitting down in the soft, clean straw.

"Where's Dinah?" called Flossie.

"Heah I is, honey lamb," answered the colored cook, as she came out with a big basket of good things to eat.

"Oh, I'm going to sit next to Dinah!" cried Bert with a laugh. "I always did like you, didn't I, Dinah?" he demanded.

"Go 'long wif you, honey!" she exclaimed.

"Yo' all doan't git none ob de stuff in dish yeah basket 'till lunch time—no, suh! No mattah how lubbin' yo' is!"

Off they started, with laughter and shouts. Uncle Daniel and his hired man sitting on the front seat, taking turns driving the horses. Freddie wanted to hold the reins, but his uncle said the animals were too frisky that morning for such little hands.

"When they come back they will be tired, and won't be so anxious to run away," the farmer said. "Then you may drive, Freddie."

All along the road were circus posters and at each new one which they saw the children would shout and laugh in delight. They saw many other farm wagons going along, also filled with family parties, who, like themselves, were going to the circus.

"Hurrah for the big show!" Bert or Nan would call out.

"Hurray! Hurray!" the children in other wagons would answer back. "Isn't it jolly?"

And indeed it was a jolly time for everyone. Even Dinah forgot her fear of the wild animals when from a distance she caught sight of the white circus tents with the gaily colored flags streaming from them.

Uncle Bobbsey found a shed, near the circus grounds, where he could leave the horses and wagon, for he did not want to take the team into town, for fear the sight of the circus animals, and the music of the band, and the steam piano, or Calliope, might scare them, and make them run away.

"We'll watch the parade," Uncle Daniel said. "Then we'll come back here, eat our lunch, and go to the show in the afternoon."

This plan was carried out, and a little later the children and the old folks were standing in line in the big crowd, waiting for the circus parade to come past. Every once in a while someone would step out into the middle of the street, and look up and down.

"Is it coming? Is it coming?" others in the crowd would ask.

"Not yet," would be the answer.

"Oh, look!" suddenly exclaimed Bert, pointing to the window of an office building near which they were standing. "There's Mr. Weston taking moving pictures!"

"Oh, so he is!" cried Nan. And there indeed, with his camera pointed out of the window, was their old friend.

He saw the children and waved to them.

"Here it comes! Here it comes!" was the sudden cry, and from the distance came the sound of music.

"The parade has started! The parade has started!" was the cry that ran through the crowd.

"Oh, isn't this great!" cried Nan, clasping her chum Mabel by the arm.

"It's just lovely!" the country girl said, "and so nice of your mother and uncle and aunt to ask me."

"Oh, we were only too glad to have you," said Nan, politely, but she meant it.

Freddie snuggled close up to fat Dinah.

"Don't you be afraid," he said to the black cook. "I—I won't let any wild animals get you!"

"Dat's a good boy, honey lamb!" she murmured, as she took hold of his hand.

Louder played the music. The children in the crowd began dancing up and down, so excited were they.

"Here it comes! Here it comes!" they cried over and over again.

Then swept past the horses, gay with plumes, and covered with blankets of gold and silver, of purple and red. On the backs of the horses rode men and women with scarlet cloaks, carrying spears tipped with glittering silver.

Then came a herd of elephants, swinging themselves along, now and then sucking up dust from the street and blowing it on their big backs to keep off the flies. Men rode on top of the elephants' heads.

"Don't be afraid! Don't be afraid, Dinah!" said Freddie over and over again.

Ponies, camels, donkeys, more horses, more elephants and other animals went past in the parade.

Then came the gilded wagons, filled with gaily dressed men and women who nodded, smiled and waved their hands at the crowds in the streets.

Bert looked up at the window where Mr. Weston was perched with his camera, and saw him taking moving pictures.

"Oh, look! There's a lion in a cage!" cried Freddie, suddenly.

Just then the big beast sent out a roar that seemed to shake the very ground, and he threw himself against the bars of his cage.

"Oh, he's going to get out! He's going to get out!" came the cry and the people rushed back away from the street.

"No danger! No danger!" shouted the circus men.

"Hold on to me, Dinah!" cried Freddie. "Hold on to me. I won't let him bite you!"

More cages of wild animals rumbled past, but most of the beasts slept peacefully Only the lion seemed to want to get out, and far down the street his roar could be heard.

"He's a new lion," said someone in the crowd. "He isn't used to being shut up, and he is trying to get out."

"Well, I hope he done stays shut up," murmured Dinah.

The parade came to an end at last, with the steam piano bringing up in the rear of the procession. The man played puffy little tunes, with a tooting chorus that made one want to dance.

"Now for lunch, and then to see the big

show," said Uncle Daniel, as he led the way back to where the wagon had been left.

And what a jolly party it was, to sit in the straw and eat nice sandwiches, pies, cookies and cakes Martha and Dinah had put into the baskets. There was lemonade, too, and if it was not pink, like the kind the circus men sold, it was much better and sweeter.

"But when are we going into the circus?" Freddie wanted to know.

"Soon now," said Uncle Daniel.

A little later they made their way to the big tents. First they went in the one where the wild animals, in cages, were drawn up in a circle inside. There were lions, tigers, bears, giraffes, rhinocerosi, hippopotami, and elephants, to say nothing of the cute monkeys.

"Are dem cages good an' strong, mistah?" asked Dinah of one of the circus attendants.

"Oh, yes," he answered, as he passed a carrot in to one of the monkeys.

"Well, dat's good," she said. "'Cause I doan't want none ob dem bears or lions t' come after me when I'se watchin' de circus performers."

"I'll see that none of them get loose," promised the circus man with a laugh at Dinah's fears.

Then the Bobbsey party went on in to the main tent. I wish I could tell you all they saw, but I have not the room in this book. There was a parade around the ring to start with, and then in came rushing the comical clowns, the men and women who rode on horses and who jumped from one trapeze to another.

Jugglers they were, men with trained horses, trick ponies, trained dogs and trained elephants. Some elephants played a ball game, others turned somersaults. Clowns jumped over their backs, and through paper hoops.

"Look here!" Nan would exclaim.

"No, see over there!" Bert would cry.

"Oh, mamma, a man jumped from the top of the tent right into a big fish net!" exclaimed Freddie.

"Look at the monkey riding on the dog's back," Flossie shouted.

"And see that man jump off a horse and jump on him again backwards!" called Tom Mason.

"Oh, but look at the cute ponies," sighed Mabel Herold.

There was so much to see and talk about that the children's eyes must have been tired, and their necks aching before the circus was over.

At last it came to an end with the exciting chariot races, and the crowd began to leave the big tent.

"Now keep close together, children," warned Mrs. Bobbsey. "You must not get lost in this crowd."

"Yes, follow me," advised Uncle Daniel.

How it happened they could not tell, but when they reached the outside of the tent, and found a space where the crowd was not so thick, Freddie was missing.

"Where is Freddie?" asked Nan, looking about for him.

"Freddie!" exclaimed her mother! "Isn't he here?"

But Freddie was not with them, and with anxious faces they looked at one another.

CHAPTER XV

FOUND AGAIN

"WHERE can he be?" asked Bert.

"I saw him but a moment ago," said Aunt Sarah.

"An' he jest had hold ob mah hand!" cried Dinah. "Oh, mah honey lamb am done et up by de ragin' lion what goes about seekin' who he kin devouer! Oh landy!"

"Quiet, Dinah, please," said Uncle Daniel. For Dinah had called out so loudly that many in the crowd turned to look at her.

"But I wants Freddie—mah honey lamb!" the loving colored woman went on. "I wants him an' he's losted!"

"We'll find him," said Uncle Daniel. "Now whom was he with when we came out of the tent?"

He had hold of my hand," said Bert, "but

he pulled away and said he wanted to walk with Dinah."

"De lubbin honey lamb!" crooned Dinah.

"Did he come with you, Dinah?" went on Uncle Daniel, trying to find out exactly who had seen Freddie last.

"Yais, sah, he done comed wif me fo' a little while in de crowd, an' den he slid away—he just seem t' melt away laik," explained the cook.

"Which way did he go?" Uncle Daniel wanted to know.

"Which way? I dunno," Dinah answered.

"Oh, perhaps he went back to the animal tent," suggested Mrs. Bobbsey. She was not really frightened as yet. Often before Freddie had been lost, but he had generally been found within a few minutes. But he had never before been lost at a circus. This time he seemed to have melted away in the big crowd.

"Let's go back to the animal tent," suggested Uncle Daniel. "Freddie was so taken with feeding the elephants peanuts that he may have gone back to do that. We'll look."

"Oh, if only dem ugly lions or tigers habn't got him!" sighed Dinah.

"The wild animals couldn't get him, 'cause they're shut up in cages, aren't they?" asked Flossie.

"Yes, dear," Nan said to her, not wanting her little sister to be frightened. "No wild animals could get Freddie."

"We'll soon find him," declared Bert.

"We'll help you look," spoke Tom Mason. "Come on, Harry."

The three boys started to push their way back through the crowd toward the animal tent.

"Now don't you three get lost," said Uncle Daniel.

"We won't!" answered Bert, "but we're going to find Freddie!"

"Oh, where can the darling be?" gasped Aunt Sarah, looking around at the crowd all about her.

"What is it? What's the matter?" asked several ladies.

"A little boy is lost—my nephew," Aunt Sarah explained.

"Oh, isn't that too bad!" cried the sympathetic ladies. "We hope you find him!"

Back into the animal tent the Bobbseys and

their relatives and friends pushed their way. It was not easy to work back through the crowd that was anxious to get away, now that the afternoon performance of the circus was over.

"He must be in there," said Uncle Daniel. "We'll find him."

Carefully he looked through the crowd of persons who were still in the animal tent. A number had remained, with their children, to get another look at the elephants, lions and tigers. Men were feeding some of the animals, now that there was a little quiet spell, and this was interesting to the youngsters.

"He doesn't seem to be here," said Aunt Sarah, as she peered through her spectacles.

"Oh, he must be!" exclaimed Mrs. Bobbsey. "He can't have gone on ahead of us, and if he turned back he would have to come into this tent."

"Oh, isn't it too bad!" exclaimed Nan, looking at her brother Bert, as though he could help. But Bert, Harry and Tom, though they had quickly made a round of the circle of animal cages, had come back to say that they found no trace of Freddie.

"I know what to do, mamma," spoke up Flossie.

"What, dear?" asked her mother, hardly knowing what she was saying.

"We ought to get a policeman," went on Flossie. "Policemans can find losted people. One found me once."

"That isn't a bad idea," spoke Uncle Daniel. "I think perhaps I had better speak to some of the town constables who are on duty here."

"Suppose we look in the big main tent," said Tom Mason. "Freddie may have wandered back in there to try and turn a somersault on one of the trapezes."

"Yes, it wouldn't do any harm to take a look," agreed Uncle Daniel. "We'll go in the big tent."

Into that large canvas house they went. Men were busy putting away some of the articles used for the animal tricks, and the balls, hoops knives and things the Japanese jugglers had used.

"Oh, where can he be?" murmured Mrs. Bobbsey.

"Something the matter, ma'am?" asked the ring-master, in his shiny tall hat, as he cracked his long whip. "Is someone lost?"

"Yes, my little boy Freddie, and we are so worried about him!"

"Well, don't worry," said the ring-master kindly. "Boys, and girls too, are lost every day at our circus performances, but they are always found all right. Don't worry. I'll have some of the men hunt for him. And you folks come with me. It's just possible he has been found and taken to the lost tent."

"The lost tent!" exclaimed Uncle Daniel. "Have you lost a tent, too?"

"No, but we have a sort of headquarters tent, or office, where all lost children are taken as soon as the circus men find them. A woman in the tent takes care of the little ones until their folks come for them. Your boy may be there waiting for you."

To the lost tent went the Bobbseys. They found two or three youngsters there, crying for their fathers or mothers, but Freddie was not among them.

"Oh, he isn't here!" cried Mrs. Bobbsey, and tears were in her eyes now. "I wish his father were here," she went on. "He would know what to do."

"Now don't you worry, ma'am," said the ring-master again. "We'll surely find him for you. He may have gone in one of the side shows, to see the fat lady, or the strong man. I'll have those places searched for you."

The ring-master did send some of his men to look in the side-show tents, but they came back to say that no one like Freddie had been seen. By this time Mrs. Bobbsey and Aunt Sarah were almost frantic with fright. Nan was crying, and even Bert, brave as he was, looked worried. A number of persons who had come to the circus offered to help look for Freddie, but, though they searched all over, the little fat fellow could not be found.

"Oh, dear! What shall we do!" cried Mrs. Bobbsey.

"Dat ugly ole lion——" began Dinah, when Nan gave a scream.

"Oh, what is it, child?" asked Aunt Sarah.

"Look. There's Freddie!" cried Nan. "There he comes!" and she pointed to her little brother being led toward them by a boy about Bert's age.

CHAPTER XVI

FRANK'S STORY

THEY all gazed in the direction in which Nan pointed. The crowd of visitors to the circus was thinnng out now, and down toward the edge of a little creek could be seen the missing Freddie walking along, his hand thrust trustingly into that of the strange boy.

"Why—why!" began Bert. "That fellow—that boy—he——" and then he stopped. Bert was not exactly sure of what he was going to say.

"Oh, Freddie!" cried Mrs. Bobbsey, running forward. "Where have you been! Such a start as you've given us! Where were you?"

But Freddie himself did not seem as anxious to rush into his mother's arms as she was to clasp him. He plodded along with the strange boy, looking quite content, and as if he wondered what all the fuss was about.

"Dere de honey lamb am!" exclaimed black

Dinah, a grin spreading over her face. "De ole lion didn't cotch him after all. Dere's mah honey lamb!"

"Freddie! Freddie!" cried Flossie, who had been resting in Uncle Daniel's arms, "did a lion eat you, Freddie? Did he?"

"A lion eat him? Of course not!" laughed Bert. And Bert was doing some hard thinking as he stared at the strange boy who had Freddie by the hand.

"I thought we should find him," said Uncle Daniel. "I knew he couldn't be lost with all these circus people around. I say!" called Mr. Bobbsey's brother to one of the men who had been helping hunt for the missing boy. "Just tell them that we found him, will you, please? Freddie's found."

"Yes, sir, I'll tell 'em," said the man. "I'm glad he's all right. I'll tell 'em!"

"But where were you, Freddie?" asked his mother, who by this time had him safely in her arms "Oh, where were you?"

"I found him down by the edge of the creek, watching 'em water the elephants," explained the strange boy, who, Mrs. Bobbsey thought, had a good, kind face. "You see, we water the elephants every afternoon when the show is over," the boy went on, "and it was down there I found him."

"Oh, I can't thank you enough for bringing him back to us," said Mrs. Bobbsey. "You were so good!"

"I didn't know just where he belonged," the strange boy explained. "But he told me his name, and where he lived, and of course I knew I could send word to his folks, though I didn't see, at first, how he got here all the way from Lakeport."

"Oh, we are visiting at his uncle's farm at Meadow Brook," explained Mrs. Bobbsey.

"So he said," went on the boy. "I was bringing him to the lost tent, when he spied you and said you were his folks."

"And I saw 'em water the elephants!" cried Freddie, struggling to get loose from his mother's arms. "The elephant sucked the water up into his nose, ma, and then he squirted it down his throat just like my fire engine squirts water. Only, 'course an elephant squirts lots more water than my engine. But

I'm goin' to get a bigger one that squirts as much as a elephant, that's what I goin' to do. And I saw one elephant, ma, he went right out in the water and laid down in it. What do you think of that!"

"The elephants often do that, ma'am," explained the strange boy. "They like to get a bath now and then, but we don't often have time to give it to them."

"You speak as though you belonged to the circus," said Uncle Daniel.

"I do," answered the boy. "That is, I'm with one of the side-shows, and I help around when there's nothing else to do."

"Well, it was very kind of you to bring back my little boy," went on Mrs. Bobbsey. Freddie was busy telling Flossie all the wonderful things he had seen.

"Oh, I didn't do anything, ma'am," the boy said. "I sort of knew this little fellow."

"You knew him?" questioned Uncle Daniel.

"Well, that is I'd seen him before."

"But I can't understand how Freddie became lost," said Mrs. Bobbsey, while Uncle

Daniel was wondering where the strange boy had seen Freddie before. "How did you get lost, Freddie?" his mother asked him.

"Lost! I wasn't lost!" he exclaimed. "I knew where I was all the time. I was with the elephants. It was you who got lost, mamma—you and Nan and Flossie and Bert——"

"Well, we called you lost," laughed Uncle Daniel. "But you're all right now, thanks to this boy. Do you live around here?" he asked. "I don't seem to remember you, though I know most of the folks in this section. But if you have seen Freddie before you must live around here."

"Oh, no, sir," was the answer. "I'm with the circus. But I used to live——"

"I know you now!" interrupted Bert. "You're Frank Kennedy, and I was with my father, calling on Mr. Mason, when I saw you. Freddie was with me then. Don't you remember, Freddie?" asked Bert. "This is the boy we saw—the boy we saw getting a——"

And Bert stopped. He did not want to say "shaking," for it was when Frank Kennedy was being severely shaken by Mr. Mason, on account of the bad twenty dollar bill, that the strange boy had last been seen by the Bobbsey lads. And on that occasion Frank had run away.

"Oh, now I know you!" cried Freddie, laughing.

"Yes, I am the boy you saw getting a shaking, for something that wasn't my fault!" exclaimed Frank, and his voice was hard and bitter. "I made up my mind I wouldn't stand Mr. Mason's cruel treatment any longer, so I ran away. I did see you two boys that time I got a shaking," Frank admitted. "You were in an automobile then," he went on, "and Mr. Bobbsey was with you." He looked around as though in search of the twins' father.

"Mr. Bobbsey had to go back to Lakeport on business," explained Mrs. Bobbsey. "We came over from Meadow Brook to the circus here to-day. And I remember Mr. Bobbsey speaking of you. So you ran away?"

"Yes'm, I ran away. I couldn't stand it in that lumber office any longer the way Mr. Mason treated me. It wasn't fair. And I'm never going back again, either. I don't like him, and he doesn't like me. I'll never let him be my guardian again."

"Poor boy!" murmured Mrs. Bobbsey "You must have had a hard time. Did you come with this circus as soon as you ran away?"

"No'm, I had a pretty bad spell first along. When I ran away I had only the clothes I wore, and only a little money. It was my own!" he said, quickly, lest they think he might have taken it from Mr. Mason's lumber office. But one look at Frank's face showed that he was honest.

"What did you do?" asked Uncle Daniel.

"Well, I walked as far as I could the first night," Frank said, going on with his story. "Then I crawled in a barn to sleep."

"Didn't you have anything to eat?" asked Nan softly. She felt very sorry for the boy.

"Well, I had a couple of crackers I had saved from my lunch that day," he explained. "Then near the barn was a cow, and I milked her. That and the crackers was all I had for supper. But I slept good in the hay."

"I had a good sleep in some hay!" exclaimed Freddie, as he remembered the time they had played hide-and-go-seek in the barn.

"It makes a good bed when you're tired," said Frank.

"What did you have for breakfast?" asked Flossie. "I like an orange and oatmeal for mine."

"Well, I didn't have anything like that for mine," explained Frank with a smile. "I didn't have much of anything the first morning. I tramped on, and finally I found a place where I could chop some wood, and a lady gave me some bread and milk. It tasted very good."

"How did you get with the circus?" asked Bert. That part interested him more than how Frank got something to eat.

"Well, I just happened to come to the town where the circus was giving a show," explained Frank. "I was around when the men were watering the horses and other animals, and I helped carry water. Then one of the men asked me if I didn't want work, and I said I did. I was hungry then, too, and I could smell the things cooking in the circus kitchen tent.

So I went to work for this show, and I've been here ever since. It's better than working in a lumber office when you get shook up every now and then," he added with a smile.

"And do you still help water the elephants?" asked Uncle Daniel.

"Oh, no, I help take tickets at one of the side shows," explained Frank. "The one where the fat lady and snakes are. I like it, though sometimes I help water the animals when I have nothing else to do. The circus people are good to me. I've earned enough money to get some clothes, and I'm never hungry any more. I was pretty ragged when I came to the circus, for I had been tramping around sleeping in barns, or wherever I could."

"Wouldn't it have been better to have gone back to Mr. Mason, your guardian?" asked Mrs. Bobbsey, for she had heard her husband tell of the time he, Bert and Freddie had seen the boy shaken before he ran away.

"Oh, no'm!" Frank exclaimed. "I'm never going back to that lumber office. Mr. Mason accused me of losing twenty dollars for him. Well, perhaps I did, but it wasn't my fault that the man gave me bad money that looked like good. I'm never going back!"

"Well, I don't know as I blame you," said Uncle Daniel softly, "but a circus is no place for a young boy. It's a hard life."

"Are you going to stay with this show?" asked Mrs. Bobbsey.

"Until I can get something better to do," answered Frank. "I know it isn't a good business, but I'll stay here until I can save some money, and then I'll look for something better. But I'll have to stay here for a while."

"Maybe you could give him work on the farm," suggested Aunt Sarah to her husband in a whisper. "I don't like him to be with a circus. And he was so good to Freddie that we ought to do something for him."

"He's too young to work on a farm," replied Uncle Daniel. "And he might be in a worse place than this circus. But we must be starting back home. It's getting late."

Freddie was hugged and kissed by his sisters, mother and aunt, and Mrs. Bobbsey insisted on making Frank a little present of money, for his kindness to Freddie. Frank did not want to take it, but finally he did.

"I'll buy some new shoes with it," he said.

"I shall tell my husband how good you were to find Freddie," said Mrs. Bobbsey, "and I am sure he will want to do something for you. I wish you would write to me once in a while. We should like to keep track of you."

"I will," promised the boy, as he put down the Bobbsey address. "I expect to be with this circus all summer," he said, as Freddie and the other children bade him good-bye.

CHAPTER XVII

A WILD ANIMAL SCARE

BACK to the shed where they had left the horses, went the Bobbsey party, the children talking on the way of the wonderful things they had seen in the circus, while the older folks spoke of Freddie being lost, and found again, by Frank Kennedy.

"But I wasn't lost!" the little chap insisted. "I knew where I was all the time. Besides, the elephants were with me, and so was Frank, the boy who was shooked. I saw him shooked and so did Bert, didn't you?" and Freddie looked at his older brother.

"Well, we won't talk about that part of it," said his mother with a smile. "It isn't nice to think about, and I am glad Frank is in a place now where he will be kindly treated. Though perhaps Mr. Mason did not mean to be cruel. He was probably very sorry at losing so much money."

"I like Frank," said Freddie. "He let me take hold of one of the elephant's tooths."

"Oh, Freddie!" exclaimed Dinah. "It's a wonder he didn't cotch an' bite yo', honey lamb!"

"Oh, I didn't take hold of one of his tooths away back in his mouth," explained Freddie, "it was the long tooth-pick tooth that stuck out under his nose."

"He means the elephant's tusk," explained Bert with a laugh.

"Oh, Freddie! I hope you weren't in any danger!" his mother cried.

"What an escape he had!" sighed Aunt Sarah. "Suppose an elephant had eaten him!"

"Pooh! Elephants don't eat anything but hay," said Freddie, who, of course, did not mean to be impolite, speaking to his aunt that way. "Frank told me so," he went on, "and I saw them eat hay. They eat a awful lot, and one of them took all my peanuts."

"Well, I'll buy you some more," said Uncle Daniel with a laugh. "You deserve it after the trouble you have had—getting lost and all that."

"I—I wasn't losted!" declared Freddie again. "I knew——"

"Oh, look at the balloons!" cried Flossie, as she saw a man outside the circus grounds selling the red, green and yellow gas-bags. "I want one, mamma!" cried the little girl.

"And so do I!" added Freddie, forgetting what he was going to say about not being lost. "I want a balloon!"

They each had one, and then the children and older folks took their places in the wagon, and soon were on their way to Meadow Brook farm again, talking over the wonderful good time they had had.

"I'm coming to the circus to-morrow," announced Freddie, as though going to circuses was all there was to do in this world.

"The circus won't be there," said Bert.

"Won't be there? Where will it go?" asked Freddie, wonderingly.

"It will travel to the next town," Bert went on. "A circus stays in a town only one day, unless it's a very big place. This show will be far away by this time to-morrow."

"And will Frank be away, too?" asked

Flossie. "I like Frank, 'cause he found Freddie."

"Yes, Frank will be away, too, poor boy," said Mrs. Bobbsey, "that is, if he stays with the circus. I wish Richard could do something for him," she went on to Uncle Daniel and Aunt Sarah. "I feel sure that boy ought to be back in his guardian's home."

"But he said Mr. Mason was cruel to him," declared Aunt Sarah.

"Perhaps he wouldn't be any more," remarked Mrs. Bobbsey, wondering how anyone could be really cruel to children. She loved her twins very much.

"Well, I'se glad mah honey lamb am safe!" murmured Dinah, as she cuddled Freddie up in her big arms.

"Oh—oh, Dinah!" cried the little fellow with a laugh. "You squeeze me like an elephant's trunk!"

"Dat's 'cause I lubs yo', honey lamb!" went on the dear old colored woman.

Back to Meadow Brook in the cool of the evening came the Bobbseys and their friends. Tom and Mabel declared they had never had such a good time, and as for Freddie and Flossie they were too busy playing with their toy balloons to say much. But you may be sure they had enjoyed themselves, and Freddie forgot all about being lost.

On their way home the Bobbseys had met Mr. Weston with his moving picture camera. He said he had made several fine views of the circus.

"What about *our* pictures?" asked Nan. "The ones you took of us children near the school?"

"They will soon be finished," said Mr. Weston. "And when they are ready to be shown, I shall send your father word, so he may bring you, and let you look at yourselves on the white screen in our moving picture theatre. Won't you like that?"

"That will be great!" cried Bert. "I never saw myself in moving pictures."

"Nor I," said Nan.

Back in the pleasant farmhouse that evening all the happenings of the day were gone over again, until Mrs. Bobbsey, noticing that Flossie and Freddie were nodding their heads, and blinking their eyes real often, said:

"Come now, little tots, time you were in bed. To-morrow is another day."

"I'm going to take my balloon to bed with me," said Freddie.

"So am I!" exclaimed Flossie, who wanted to do as many things as did her brother.

"Oh, I wouldn't," their mother said. "Leave the balloons here until morning."

"And then we'll have a balloon race," proposed Bert.

"What's a balloon race?" Freddie wanted to know.

"No more talk to-night, little fat fireman!" said his mother. "Off to bed you go!" and he and Flossie were "packed off," the other children coming soon after.

Freddie and Flossie were up bright and early next morning, out playing with their balloons before breakfast. They tied long threads to them, and let them float above the trees.

"When will we have the balloon race?" asked Freddie.

"Whenever you like," Bert answered. "Only to have a race you have to let your balloon sail off, without any string fast to it, and you will not get it back again."

At first Freddie would not hear of that, but finally he and Flossie became tired of the toy circus balloons, and came to Bert to beg him to make a race for them.

Bert cut the string off both balloons. Freddie's was red and Flossie's blue.

"Now we'll let go of both balloons at the same time," Bert explained, "and the balloon that goes up highest will win the race. Now watch, everyone!"

They all watched, as Bert let go the toys, one from either hand. Up, up, up, went the red and blue balloons.

"Oh, mine's going faster!" cried Freddie.

"No, mine is!" exclaimed Flossie.

And, for a time first the red balloon would be ahead, and then the blue one. But finally they both were at exactly the same height, and in that way they sailed onward and upward until they were only little specks in the blue sky, so no one could tell which one was ahead in the race.

It was while the children were out in the yard in front of the Meadow Brook farmhouse, watching the disappearing balloons, that Bert heard a stranger's voice calling.

"I say, do you children know where there is a circus around here?" was the question, and, turning, Nan, Bert and the others saw a man in a carriage, on the road just outside the fence.

"A circus?" repeated Bert.

"Yes, I heard there was one showing around here," the man went on, "and I'd like to find it."

"There was a circus over at Rosedale yesterday," spoke Bert, "but it has traveled on by this time. If you inquired there you could find out where it went."

"I'll do that," the man said. "I'm much obliged to you," and he was about to drive on, when Bert asked:

"Aren't you Mr. Mason, who has a lumber yard near my father's?"

"Whoa!" called the man to his horse. "Yes, I'm Mr. Mason," he went on, "and I have a lumber yard. But I don't seem to know you."

"I'm Bert Bobbsey," the lad said, "and my father——"

"Oh, yes, to be sure! Of course I know you!" the man exclaimed. "Why, you were the boy in the automobile the day my ward, Frank Kennedy, ran away from me."

"Yes, I was there," said Bert.

"Well, it's about Frank that I came on here," said Mr. Mason. "I have been tracing him. I heard he joined a circus when he ran away from me, and I want to find him and take him back. I came on here by train, and hired this horse and carriage to drive about the country. But now, when I am almost up to the circus, you tell me it has moved. That's too bad, and I'm not sure, when I find it, that Frank will be with it."

"I think he will be, Mr. Mason," said Bert, quietly.

"What's that?' cried Mr. Mason. "You think Frank will be with the circus? What makes you think so?"

"Because we saw him with it yesterday," said Nan, taking part in the talk, "and he said he was going to travel with it."

"Yes, that's right," agreed Bert. He thought it only fair to give information about Frank, since Mrs. Bobbsey had said she thought it would be best for the runaway boy to go back to his guardian.

"Hum!" exclaimed Mr. Mason. "If Frank is with the circus, I'll soon get him. I'll drive over to Rosedale, and inquire where the show went from there. I can easily trace it. Much obliged to you for your information," he called over his shoulder, as he drove off. He did not stop to inquire how Frank was, nor how he had fared since running away. Perhaps Mr. Mason did not think of this.

"Oh, I hope he—I hope he doesn't shake Frank, when he finds him," said Nan, as the lumber man drove on.

"I don't believe he will," remarked Bert. "I fancy Frank will make his guardian promise to treat him better if he goes back to the lumber office."

Nan and Bert went in the house to tell their mother of meeting the man who was looking for Frank. She said they had done right to tell what they knew.

"Poor boy," she sighed, "he hasn't had a very happy life, but perhaps this will be all for the good, and he may be better treated now."

That afternoon, as Harry and the Bobbsey children, with Tom Mason and Mabel Herold were going down the road to pick some blackberries, they met a farmer boy driving an empty hay wagon. This boy knew Bert, Harry and Tom.

"Hello!" he called to them, "did you hear the news about the circus?"

"What news?" asked Bert, wondering if the boy meant that Mr. Mason had reached the show and taken away Frank.

"News about the wild animals escaping from the circus," went on the boy on the hay-wagon.

"Wild animals escaping!" exclaimed Nan, with a frightened look over her shoulder, while Flossie came over closer to her sister.

"That's it!" said the boy. "When the show was moving out of Rosedale last night, some tigers and lions got loose, and ran off in the woods. They looked for 'em, but couldn't find 'em. Some of the farmers around here are out now with guns."

"Oh, Nan!" exclaimed Flossie. "Let's go back home! I don't like wild animals!"

CHAPTER XVIII

WHAT FREDDIE SAW

FOR a few seconds Bert and Harry, his cousin, stared at the boy on the hay-wagon. Then Harry, who knew him well, asked:

"Say, Jim Bates, are you joking or did you really hear about some wild animals escaping from the circus?"

"Indeed I'm not joking!" cried Jim. "I did hear it! Bill Snowden told me. You know he lives over on the road that runs from Rosedale to Blaisdell and the circus went there. It went right past his house in the night, and he looked out of his window and saw the camels and elephants and wild animal cages."

"I saw the elephants, too!" exclaimed Freddie. "I took hold of one's big toothpick tooth. Elephants eat hay. Were they eating any hay when that boy saw 'em? I wish elephants would go past our house."

"Quiet, Freddie dear, please," said Nan. "We want to hear about the wild animals. Did they really get loose?" she asked, and she looked over her shoulder, as did Flossie and Mabel Herold.

"Well, that's what Bill Snowden said," replied Jim Bates. "Of course I didn't see 'em run away myself, but I'm all ready for 'em, if I meet any bears, or lions or tigers," he added.

"Ready for 'em—how do you mean?" asked Bert.

"I've got a big club, and some stones," answered Jim, and he took up from the seat beside him a stout stick, and showed where he had made a little pile of stones in the wagon.

"They wouldn't hurt a lion," said Freddie. "Lions or tigers aren't afraid of sticks or stones. I'm going to get my fire engine. It squirts water, and wild animals is afraid of water."

"Yes, we've heard that story before," said Bert, with a laugh. "But don't you go out hunting for wild animals with that toy engine of yours, Freddie!" his older brother advised.

"No, indeed," added Nan. "Oh, I think we ought to go home, Bert."

"I'm going home," said the boy on the wagon, "and if I meet any animals on the way I'm going to throw stones at 'em."

"Pooh! They won't be afraid of stones," declared Freddie.

"Yes, they will, too!" declared Jim Bates. "I read in a book that a bear's nose is very soft and tender, and if you hit him on it he'll howl and run away."

"I heard that, too," said Harry. "I hope it's true."

"Well, if a bear's nose is tender, a lion's or a tiger's must be tender also," went on Jim, "and if I meet any wild animals I'm going to hit 'em on the nose."

"That's a good idea," Bert said, with a laugh. "But how can you be sure you'll hit 'em on the nose?"

"Oh, I can't be sure," admitted Jim, "but I'm a pretty good shot throwing stones, and I've got plenty, so if I miss the first time I'll hit 'em on the nose later. There isn't any wild animal going to get me. No sir!" and he looked at the stones and his stout club.

"I should think," said Mabel Herold, "that

if you had a good team of horses you could drive fast and get away from any wild animals you might meet."

"Well, I could do that, too," replied the boy on the hay-wagon. "And if I throw all my stones, and don't hit a lion or a bear on the nose, I'll whip up and get away."

"Well, I'm going to get away now," decided Nan. "Come on, Flossie and Mabel. We won't go berrying to-day. Bears like blackberries, so I've read, and no one can tell but that there might might be one in the berry patch where we are going."

"Oh, I don't think so!" exclaimed Bert. "Maybe there isn't any truth in that story after all, about the wild animals escaping. That other boy didn't see 'em get away, did he?" asked Bert of Jim.

"No, he didn't exactly see 'em," admitted the boy on the hay-wagon, "but he heard the circus men talking in the night about how the lion and the bear and the tiger got out of their cages."

"Oh, come on home, Nan! Come on home!" begged Flossie. "This is worse than the shooting in the moving pictures. Let's go home."

Nan was very willing to go, and so was Mabel. Freddie, too, after thinking it over, decided that he had better go back with the girls, and get his toy fire engine ready for any possible danger.

"What do you say, Bert, shall we go back?" inquired Harry.

"Well, I don't know," slowly replied the older Bobbsey lad. "I don't really believe in the least that any wild animals are loose, but if the girls aren't going berrying there's no use in us going."

"I guess that's right," agreed Tom. "No use going on alone."

And, though none of the older boys would admit it, I think they, too, were rather glad to turn back after having heard the story of the escape of the wild circus animals.

"Well, I'm all ready for 'em, if I meet any," declared Jim, as he drove on, having told the news.

On the way back Bert and the others met several farmers who knew Harry or Tom, and each of these men said they had also heard the story of the escape of a lion, tiger and bear.

"And if they are loose, some of us may miss some cattle or sheep," declared Mr. Ames, who lived not far from Uncle Daniel. "I think we farmers will have to get up a hunting party."

"I'd like to come," broke in Freddie. "I've got a fire engine, and wild animals is afraid——"

"That will do, dear," said Nan, gently putting her finger across his lips. "Little boys can't go hunting wild animals."

By the time the Bobbsey twins and their friends had almost reached Meadow Brook, on their way back, they had met several persons—men or boys—who spoke of having heard of the escape of the circus animals.

When the children came up the gravel walk of the farmhouse, Mrs. Bobbsey, seeing them from the side porch, where she was sitting, stringing beans for supper, called out:

"Well you are back early. Did you get many berries?"

"We didn't get any, mother," said Nan. "We——"

"It's wild animals!" burst out Freddie, unable to keep quiet any longer. "A lion, a tiger and a bear! They got away from the circus, and they—they——"

"What's all this?" interrupted Aunt Sarah, coming out with her sewing in her hands

Then, by turns, with many interruptions from Freddie, the story was told. Dinah listened with wide-opened eyes, and if she could have turned pale I think she would have done so. But of course she could not, for she was the color of a chocolate cake, and had to stay that way.

"Oh, I don't believe a word of it!" exclaimed Uncle Daniel, when he heard the tale. "Every time a circus comes to town there is a story of wild animals escaping, but I've never seen any yet. I don't believe it at all!"

But the children did, and later, when Uncle Daniel came back from a visit to the village store that evening, he had to admit that several persons had spoken to him about the wild beasts being loose.

"Hadn't you better see if your shot gun is loaded?" his wife asked him.

"Well, I will, if it will make you feel any easier," he agreed. "But there's no danger of any of them coming near here, even if they have escaped, which I don't believe."

The children were rather frightened that night, and would not go far from the porch to play in the moonlight, which they usually did before going to bed.

Of course Bert and Harry were not as frightened as were Flossie and Freddie, but they looked nervously over their shoulders at the dark places under the bushes as they passed them.

Freddie, true to his promise, got out his toy fire engine, and filled the tank with water, winding up the spring that worked the pump and sent out the stream from the little rubber hose.

"Now I'm ready for a lion or a tiger or a bear," he said.

"Well, don't dream of them," said his mother. "Now it's time for bed."

Whether the talk of the circus animals had made Freddie nervous, or whether he did dream of them, he could not clearly tell afterward. All he knew was that he did not sleep well, and, some time after going to bed he awakened with a start.

There was no light in his room, but the moon shone in. He could look across to where Flossie was asleep in her crib.

Then Freddie heard a noise. It came from outside and sounded like: "Wuff!"

"Oh! Oh!" whispered Freddie to himself. "That's him! That's one of the wild animals! It's a bear! That's how bears go—'wuff!' Oh, it's come, and what shall I do!"

He sat up in bed listening. He heard the noise again!

"Wuff! Wuff!"

Then Freddie decided he must be brave. Without waking Flossie, the little fellow slid from bed, and crossed to the window. The bear, if such it was, could not be in his room. He was sure of that, for the place was made bright by the moonlight that streamed in the window.

Over to this window Freddie went. He looked out, and as he did so, he saw something shaggy and black walk under the lilac bush in front of the house.

"There he is!" whispered Freddie to himself. Then in his shrill childish voice he called aloud:

"Mamma! Bert! Nan! It's come! The bear! He's out in front under the bush! Oh! Oh! Oh!"

CHAPTER XIX

IN SWIMMING

FREDDIE'S cries roused the whole house at Meadow Brook, for the little Bobbsey boy had a strong, ringing voice.

His mother was suddenly awakened from her sleep in the next room. Aunt Sarah and Uncle Daniel heard him in their apartment. Nan, Bert and Harry also heard him.

"Oh, Freddie!" cried Flossie, who slept in the same room with her little brother. "What is it? What is it, Freddie?" and she sat up in her crib.

"It's a bear—out in front—under a bush. The circus bear!" answered Freddie. "I didn't see the lion or tiger, but they must be out there too, unless the bear ate them up!"

"Oh! Oh!" cried Flossie. "Oh, dear!"

"Mamma! Nan! Bert!" cried Nan. "Come, oh, come here! Dinah!"

"I'se comin', honey lamb! I'se comin'!" cried the colored cook, as she heard Freddie's wild cry. "What am de mattah, honey lamb?"

Others were asking this question now.

"What's it all about?" called Bert.

"A bear!" answered Freddie.

"Lions and tigers," added Flossie, half sobbing.

"Gracious! Freddie's been dreaming, or else he's talking in his sleep," said Bert to Harry, who was also awakened by the shouts of the little boy.

By this time Mrs. Bobbsey was up, and had put on a dressing gown and slippers. She hurried out into the hall, to meet Aunt Sarah.

"Oh, something dreadful must have happened," said Freddie's mother. But when she went in his room, she found him and Flossie safe, with the little boy standing in the moonlight, near the open window.

"What is it, little man?" asked Aunt Sarah.

"Hush! Not so loud!" cautioned Flossie "It's bears and lions and tigers. Freddie saw 'em!" She was not so frightened now.

"I did not see 'em!" cried Freddie. "I only saw a bear!"

"Oh, yes, the bear ate the lion and tiger," went on Flossie, "and if Snap or Snoop would only eat the bear now, it would be all right."

"What does it all mean?" asked Mrs. Bobbsey. "Did you really see something, Freddie, or were you dreaming?"

"I did see something, mamma, and it went: 'Wuff! Wuff!'" Freddie explained. "Then it went and hid under the lilac bush. I'll show you," and, taking his mother's hand, he led her to the window, out of which he pointed.

Now Nan, Bert and Harry came into the small twins' room.

"What is it?" they asked.

By turns Flossie and Freddie told their story, Freddie doing the "Wuff! Wuff!" part very earnestly, until Flossie begged him to stop, as he "skeered" her.

Dinah, too, came waddling into the room, bringing a candle which dripped grease down on her bare feet. The grease was hot, and as Dinah felt it, she gave a yell which was almost as startling as was Freddie's.

"Oh, what is it?" cried Mrs. Bobbsey.

"Candle grease done splashed on mah toe, an' burnt me," Dinah explained, as she stood on one foot, and held the other on top of it to ease the pain.

"There it is! There it is!" suddenly cried Freddie. "There's the bear!" and he leaned so far out of the window that Bert had to catch his little brother by his night gown to save him from a possible fall.

Mrs. Bobbsey and Aunt Sarah looked out, and saw a big black object come into the moonlight.

"Oh, it *is* a bear!" declared Mrs. Bobbsey.

"It does look like some strange beast," agreed Aunt Sarah.

"I wish Mr. Bobbsey were here," said the lumber merchant's wife.

"Uncle Daniel will fix him!" declared Freddie. "Uncle Daniel's got a gun. Mamma, can't I take my fire engine and squirt water on that bear?"

"No, indeed!" answered Mrs. Bobbsey. "Get back to bed right away."

"Dan, you'd better see what it is,' said Aunt

Sarah, as her husband, half dressed, was heard out in the hall. "There *is* some animal under the lilac bush."

"I'll soon have him out of that," said the farmer. He had his gun with him, and while the children watched from the window, they saw him step out of the kitchen door.

"Oh, he's going to shoot!" cried Freddie in a shrill whisper, as he watched his uncle.

"I don't want to hear him!" murmured Flossie, as she got into her crib, and pulled the bed clothes over her ears.

But Bert, Nan and the others watched. Then, just as Uncle Daniel raised the gun, to shoot at something black which he saw beneath the lilac bush, an animal rushed out, and gave a howl.

Hardly had that died away than there sounded a loud:

"Bow! Wow! Wow!" This was repeated several times.

"Oh, it's only a dog!" cried Bert.

"Is it Snap?" Freddie wanted to know.

"No, it's a big black stray dog," answered Bert.

"No wonder Freddie thought it was a bear," said Mrs. Bobbsey. "Now it's all over, go back to bed, and sleep in peace."

And it was only a dog that had caused all the excitement. The animal ran out into the moonlight, stood a moment looking at Uncle Daniel with the gun, and then gave more barks.

It was as if he said he did not like to be chased away in that fashion.

"Well, it's a good thing I didn't shoot him," said Uncle Daniel as he came back into the house.

"Whose dog was it?" asked his wife.

"Snook's big black one. He was hunting for a bone, I guess, and he must have sniffed and snuffed when the dirt got up his nose. That woke Freddie. It was only a dog."

"Only a dog!" murmured Freddie. "I thought it was a bear!"

"Well, I'm glad it wasn't, or a tiger or lion, either," said Flossie, as she curled up in her cot.

Soon the house was quiet again, and everyone went to sleep. In the morning Freddie and Flossie went out to look at the place under the lilac bush where the dog had been seen. They found a hole where he had been digging up a bone he had hidden there.

And, a little later that day, the dog himself came over, to make friends with Snap. He let Freddie pat him.

"He isn't half as big as he looked in the night," said the little fellow.

"No, daylight often makes many things seem smaller—even troubles, that look very big at night," said Mrs. Bobbsey, with a smile.

"But maybe we'll see some wild animals that got away from the circus," hopefully said Freddie at dinner.

"No, you won't!" exclaimed his uncle with a laugh.

"Why not?" asked Bert.

"Because none got away," was the answer. "I met one of the circus men in the village this morning. He stayed behind to settle up some bills, and he said not a single animal got away. It was all a false alarm; no truth in it."

"Well, I'm glad of it!" declared Mrs. Bobbsey, and I think everyone felt better on hearing that news.

Mr. Bobbsey came back to Meadow Brook the next day, and heard all about the wild animal scare, and also about Freddie being lost at the circus, and Frank Kennedy finding him.

"And Mr. Mason is looking for Frank at the circus, wherever the show is now," said Bert.

"Yes, so I heard," remarked Mr. Bobbsey. "Well, I hope he treats the poor boy kindly if he takes him back."

It was a hot, quiet summer afternoon, a few days later, tnat Bert and Harry, with Tom Mason, sat under the trees in front of the farmhouse. Mrs. Bobbsey and Aunt Sarah had gone calling, Flossie and Freddie were asleep in the house, and Nan had gone over to see Mabel Herold.

"What can we do?" asked Bert, stretching his arms.

"I don't want to do much except keep cool," spoke Harry.

"That's what I say!" exclaimed Tom. "And I know a good way to get that way, too."

"What way?" asked Bert, closing his eyes

"Cool. Let's go swimming. It's just right for that!"

"All right!" agreed Harry.

"Fine!" cried Bert. "Let's do it."

A little later they were on their way to the old swimming hole, near the willow tree that grew on the edge of the brook or little river.

CHAPTER XX

FRANK COMES BACK

"WATCH me dive in!"

"I can swim under water!"

"Let's see who can first swim across to the other side of the big hole!"

Bert Bobbsey, his cousin Harry, Tom Mason and some other boys were standing on the bank of the little brook, or river, as it was sometimes called, all ready for a cool bath that hot summer day. The water of the "old swimming hole," as it was called, was not deep enough to be dangerous, and Mrs. Bobbsey was not afraid to have Bert go there without his father. Bert's father had taught him to swim.

"All ready now?" asked Harry, as the boys stood in line on the edge of the little pool, waiting for the dive.

"All ready!" answered Bert.

"Then go!" cried the farm-boy.

Into the water they splashed, head first, disappearing under the waves. Up they bounced again, like corks, and then they began swimming for the other side.

"A race! A race!" cried Bert, shaking his head to get the water out of his eyes and nose. He had held his mouth tightly shut when diving, so no water had been able to get between his lips.

"I'll race you!" exclaimed Tom Mason, and soon the boys were swimming as hard as they could toward the other bank. Some of them could not swim very well, but they paddled, or swam "dog-fashion."

"Tom's going to win!" cried one of the boys who could not swim fast. He was now standing up in the water, looking at the three boys in the lead.

"No, I think Bert will get to the other side first!" said another boy, who stood on the bank, not yet having dived in.

"You're all wrong, Harry will beat!" exclaimed a third boy, and so it proved. Harry soon passed Bert and Tom, and reached the farther bank first. Then Tom came next, while poor Bert was last.

"Too bad you couldn't win," said Harry kindly.

"Oh, you two are better swimmers than I am," said Bert. "I don't mind being beaten that way. I guess I need more practice."

"That's it," his cousin said. "I have had more chances to swim than you do, so of course I ought to be better."

"You can beat me, and I swim as much as you do," said Tom, who had lived in the country all his life, and near the little river. "I used to beat Harry every time," said Tom to Bert, "but now he goes ahead of me."

"Well, maybe you'll beat him next time," remarked Bert, with a laugh.

After the little race the boys swam about as they pleased, now jumping in, or diving head first from the bank near the deeper part of the pool, sometimes swimming under water, and then jumping out to lie in the warm sand, or on the green grass.

"Oh, this is great fun!" exclaimed Bert, as he sat on the edge of the bank, swinging his bare feet to and fro. "I'm glad we came!"

"Look out!" suddenly called Tom, but he spoke too late. Just then Harry slipped quietly up behind Bert and pushed him into the water.

"Whoop!" yelled Bert, as he splashed in. He went under, but soon came up again, and, swimming to shore, crawled out.

"You wait until I get hold of you!" he cried laughingly to Harry. "I'll toss you in! Just wait!"

"You've got to get me first!" replied Harry, keeping out of Bert's way. Bert raced after Harry but did not catch him. However, Bert waited his chance and a little later, when he saw Harry sitting on the edge of the hole, talking to one of the other boys, Bert stole softly up behind his cousin, and pushed him into the water.

"Wow!" cried Harry as he splashed in.

"Now we're even," Bert said with a laugh.

After this the boys played some games in the water, swimming about, "ducking" one another, and having lots of fun.

"Well, I guess it's about time we started

for home," said Harry, after a bit, as he noticed the sun, like a ball of fire, sinking to rest in the western sky. "I'll have to go after the cows soon."

"I'll go with you," offered Bert, as the boys came out of the water, and began to dress.

They were almost ready to start back home when Bert noticed a boy walking along the path that extended on one side of the river.

At first Bert did not pay much attention to the boy, after giving him one glance, but as the strange lad came nearer Bert looked at him more closely.

"I wonder where I've seen that boy before?" he said aloud.

"What boy?"

"Over there," replied Bert, pointing.

Harry gave one look, and exclaimed:

"Why, don't you remember? That's the boy who found Freddie when he was lost at the circus!"

"Oh, so it is!" exclaimed Bert. "But what is he doing here? Why isn't he with the show?"

"I don't know," answered Harry, who was

trying to untangle a hard knot in his shoe lace. "Better ask him."

"I will, if he comes near enough," decided Bert, as he finished dressing. Then he "ruffled" up his hair, so it would dry more quickly.

By this time they had on their clothes, and the other boy had noticed the lads who had just finished swimming. He gave them one look, and then turned hurriedly away, as if he did not want them to see him.

"Hold on wait a minute—Frank!" called Bert.

The boy stopped as he heard his name mentioned.

"Who wants me?" he asked.

"I do—Bert Bobbsey," was the answer. "You know me. You found my little brother Freddie, when he was lost at the circus. Don't you remember?"

"Oh—yes," was the answer.

The boy walked slowly forward, and as he came nearer Bert could see that he looked tired and hungry.

"What's the matter?" Harry asked. "Why

aren't you with the circus any more? Did you lose your place?"

"Well, no, not exactly," replied Frank, "but the side show I worked for busted up— I mean it failed, and I was out of a place. There was nothing else for me to do in the circus, so I had to leave it. I haven't any work now, and I don't know what to do."

"That's too bad," said Bert kindly. "What are you going to do?"

"I don't know," and Frank's voice was sad.

"Are you going back to the lumber office?" asked Harry, for he had heard his cousin tell how Frank had run away from his guardian, Mr. Mason, who punished the boy for taking in a Confederate twenty dollar bill, that was worthless.

"No, I'll never go back there!" exclaimed Frank, with flashing eyes.

"Mr. Mason was looking for you, the day after the circus showed in Rosedale," said Bert. "Did he see you?"

"No, he didn't, and I don't want to see him," Frank said. "After I lost my place in the side show, where I took in tickets at the tent entrance, I started to tramp, and look for work. But I haven't found any yet. So I thought I'd come back to Meadow Brook. I heard there were some farms around here, and I thought maybe I could get work on one of them. If I can't—I don't know what to do," and it sounded as if Frank was trying to keep from crying.

CHAPTER XXI

BAD MONEY

BERT, Harry and their chums hardly knew what to do. They felt sorry for Frank, and wanted to help him, but they did not know just how to go about it.

"Do you know how to work on a farm?" asked Harry.

"Well, no, not exactly," replied Frank. "But I know something about the lumber business, and I guess I could chop wood. They have to do that on farms, don't they?" he asked, and he was smiling a little now.

"Oh, yes, wood has to be chopped," said Harry. "Entirely too much of it, I think. It makes my back ache."

"Say, why can't we ask him to come back with us?" whispered Bert to Harry, as Frank picked up a stone and tossed it into the water.

"I guess we could," said Harry, slowly.

"Then I'm going to do it," went on Bert. "I say," he spoke to Frank, "wouldn't you like to come back to my uncle's house, and get something to eat? Maybe he could give you work. I know Harry and I have plenty to do."

"I would like to come, very much," replied Frank, a brighter look coming over his face. "I'll do all the work I can, too," he added, quickly.

"Come along then," invited Harry, and as Bert and Frank walked along together, ahead of the others, Harry told his chums how he had first met Frank at the circus, the time Freddie was lost. He also explained to the boys what Bert had told him about Frank running away.

Leaving their chums with whom they had gone swimming, Bert and Harry led Frank down toward the pleasant farmhouse. Freddie was out in front, playing with his toy fire engine as usual. As soon as the little Bobbsey twin saw the circus lad, he exclaimed:

"Oh, there's my boy—my elephant-boy that found me when everybody was lost but me. Oh, I'm glad to see you!" he cried, and he ran to Frank, who caught Freddie up in his arms, and kissed him.

Nan and Flossie came down off the porch to see what all the excitement was about.

"Oh, it's the circus-boy!" Flossie cried. "Did you bring any trained monkeys or elephants with you?" she asked.

"No, not this time, I'm sorry to say," replied Frank. "They wouldn't let me take any of the animals with me when I came away."

"Well, did you bring any—any peanuts?" asked Freddie. "Peanuts are good, even if you haven't any elephants to eat 'em."

"No peanuts, either," went on Frank. Poor lad! He looked so hungry that if he had had any peanuts he probably would have eaten them himself.

"Well, did you bring any—any balloons?" Flossie wanted to know.

"Well, yes, I have some toy balloons," said Frank, and he pulled some pieces of rubber from his pocket. "These are circus balloons before they are blown up," explained Frank. "You can use a hollow goose quill to blow them full of air, and then tie a string, or thread, around the bottom, so the air won't come out. They won't go up like circus balloons, though," Frank said.

"Why not?" Freddie wanted to know.

"Because they have only air in them, instead of gas," Frank explained. "Gas is lighter than air, and that makes it lift the balloon. But you can have some fun with these," and he gave two each to Flossie and Freddie. "One of the circus men gave them to me," he went on. The children were soon playing with the balloons.

By this time Mrs. Bobbsey had come out of the house, and when she saw Frank she remembered him at once.

"Oh, it is very good to see you again," she exclaimed, and she looked sorry when he told her he had lost his place with the circus.

"Well, perhaps it is all for the best," said Mr. Bobbsey, when he heard the news. "A circus is not the nicest place in the world for a growing boy, though many good men and women are in circuses."

"I think I'd like to work on a farm for a change," said Frank.

"Well, you won't find farm work very easy," spoke Uncle Daniel, as he came out to listen to the runaway's story. "And I think you had better go back to your guardian," he added. "He has been looking for you."

"So Bert said," remarked Frank, "but I'll never go back to that lumber office to be treated as I was before. Mr. Mason really wasn't fair to me."

"Perhaps he meant to be," said Mr. Bobbsey.

"Well, didn't he punish me for something that wasn't my fault—taking that bad twenty dollar bill?" asked Frank.

"He did punish you, yes," admitted Mr. Bobbsey, "and I am not saying he did right in that. But you were put in his charge by the courts, and he has authority to look after you, the same as a father would look after his children."

"I think it is best that you go back to him," went on Uncle Daniel.

"I never will!" exclaimed Frank.

"Would you if I saw Mr. Mason and got him to promise to treat you more kindly, and overlook the loss of the twenty dollars?" asked the farmer.

"Well, I might," replied Frank, slowly.

"That's better!" exclaimed Uncle Daniel. "I like a young lad to have a real home," he went on, "and not be traveling about with a circus, no matter how good a show it is. What happened to the side-show you were with?" he asked Frank.

"Oh, our biggest snake died," said the boy, "and the fat lady was taken sick, and got so thin she wasn't a curiosity any more, so the show 'busted up,' as the circus people called it."

"Well, maybe it's just as well," said Mrs. Bobbsey. "I never did like snakes, anyhow, and it can't be healthful to be as fat as that lady was. I hope she gets better, and is thin enough to be comfortable. And now we must look after you, Frank. You will stay with us a few days, until Mr. Bobbsey and Uncle Daniel can arrange about your going back to your guardian."

"Yes," said Mr. Bobbsey. "Now that you have promised, Frank, I shall write to Mr.

Mason, telling him you are here. He is probably searching for you, wondering what has happened to you since you lost your place with the circus."

"You are very kind to me," murmured the homeless boy.

"Yes, and I think Mr. Mason will be kind to you, too, after we have had a talk with him," said Mr. Bobbsey. "Now, Frank, make yourself at home here, and have a good time."

Frank certainly needed a good time if anyone did, for he had not had much fun thus far in life.

Aunt Sarah took Frank to the dining-room, and soon Dinah had served a meal that would make any hungry boy feel very much at home, Frank said

"He shore hab got some appetite!" exclaimed Dinah, as she looked in through a crack in the kitchen door, and watched Frank eat.

"Well, I guess anyone would have an appetite if they had to live on hay and oats," said Martha.

"Hay an' oats!" cried Dinah. "Did he hab t' eat hay an' oats?"

"He must have," Martha replied. "That's about all they have in circuses."

"Pore boy!" sighed Dinah. "I'se gwine t' bake him a whole chocolate cake fo' his ownse'f; dat's what I am!"

And she did, too, though Frank shared his treat with the others, a day or so later, when it was given to him.

Meanwhile Frank was taken in almost as one of the family by the Bobbseys and their relatives and friends. Freddie never wanted to be away from his "circus-boy," as he called Frank, and Flossie, too, was quite in love with the wanderer.

"It makes me homesick for Mrs. Mason's two little girls," said Frank to Mrs. Bobbsey, as he came in one day from having taken Freddie and Flossie for a walk.

"Well, it's a good sign to be homesick," said Mrs. Bobbsey. "It shows you like your home, in spite of some bad times there. You will soon be back again."

Mr. Mason had been written to, and told that his ward was at Meadow Brook, and would go back with him if he called. But no answer had yet been received.

"I suppose he is trying to find you by following up the circus," said Mr. Bobbsey to Frank.

A few days after this Bert, Harry and Frank were on their way to the village store to get some groceries for Aunt Sarah. As they came near the place, in front of which was a large porch, a man was seen peering around the corner of the building. At the sight of him Frank started and pulled Bert by the sleeve.

"What's the matter?" asked Harry's cousin.

"That man!" whispered Frank. "See him! That's the one who gave me the bad money—the Confederate twenty dollar bill. What can he be doing here? Oh, if I could only get Mr. Mason's money back from that man!"

"Let's wait and see what he is doing," suggested Harry. The man had not yet seen them. The boys could watch him as he seemed to be hiding back of the corner of the country store.

"He's up to some trick, I'm sure," said Bert.

A few seconds later Mr. Mack, the owner of the store, came out and walked down the village street. Hardly had he started off than the strange man quickly went into the store.

"He's going to take the money!" exclaimed Bert. "There's no one in the store now. He waited for Mr. Mack to come out, so he could go in and get the money."

"No, I don't think that," spoke Harry. "George Smith, a boy I know, works for Mr. Mack, and attends to the store when Mr. Mack goes out. George must be in there now."

"Well, that man is up to some trick, I'm sure!" exclaimed Frank. "How can we find out what it is?"

"We can go in the store through the back door," said Harry. "Come on, we'll do it, and sneak in quietly! Then we can see what's going on."

Quietly the three boys went into the store through the rear entrance. No one up front could see them because of the piles of boxes and barrels in front of the counters.

"Well, what can I do for you to-day?" the three heard George Smith ask the stranger.

"I want two pounds of the best butter," was the man's answer. "And I suppose you can change a twenty dollar bill, can't you?"

"Oh, yes," said George. "We've got that much change."

"You were sure of that?" asked the man, glancing around the store nervously.

"Yes, sir, we always keep plenty of change on hand."

"Very well then, go and weigh out the butter and be sure and give me good weight."

"We always give full weight, sir," answered George.

Bert and the others could hear, but could not see George as he weighed out the butter. Then Frank whispered:

"I want to get near enough so I can see what kind of a twenty dollar bill that man gives this boy. Maybe it will be no good, just as he fooled me."

"Come over here," whispered Harry. "You can look through this crack between two boxes. It's right near the cash drawer, and you can see the bill when George makes change for it."

Frank crept up to make an observation, and

as the store boy took the bill from the man, and began making change, Frank could not hold back any longer. He saw that the bill was the same kind that had fooled him. It was Confederate money, and utterly worthless.

"Don't give that man any change!" cried Frank. "That's bad money!"

CHAPTER XXII

HAPPY DAYS

Bert and Harry were so surprised at Frank's sudden call, that, for a few seconds, they did not know what to do or say. George Smith, the boy in the store, was also startled. He stood with the bad twenty dollar bill in his hand, wondering where the warning voice had come from. And then Frank showed how quick he could be.

"Hurry up!" he whispered to Bert and Harry. "One of you slip around and lock the front door, and the other one lock the back. Then we'll have this man trapped, and maybe I can make him pay back the money he got from me. Quick!"

"I'll go to the front door!" exclaimed Harry.

"And I'll lock the back one!" said Bert.

The man, who had heard Frank's call from

behind the pile of boxes, must have known something had gone wrong with his plan to cheat.

"Never mind about the butter," he said quickly. "I guess I won't buy any after all. Just give me back my twenty dollar bill, and I'll get along."

"Oh, no, you won't!" exclaimed Harry, as he slipped around some barrels. Quickly running to the front door, the country boy locked it, and stood in front of it.

"Hurry! Give me my money back, I tell you!" cried the man to George, who stood near the cash drawer, not knowing what to do.

"Don't you give it to him!" advised Frank, stepping out. "Lock the back door, Bert," he called.

"I have!" cried the older Bobbsey boy.

The man started to run behind the counter, to find a way out, but he was too late. Bert had locked the door, and taken out the key.

"Let me out of here!" cried the stranger. "Let me out!"

Bert and Harry were somewhat frightened, but Frank was brave.

"You don't get out of here until you pay back the twenty dollars you cheated out of Mr. Mason," he said.

"I don't know anything about any Mr. Mason!" the stranger said. "I want my twenty dollar bill back, I won't need any butter to-day!"

"Don't give him that money!" cried Frank to George. "It's bad, and if you give it to him, he'll try to cheat someone else with it."

"I'll fix you!" cried the man. But at that instant there was a rattling sound at the front door, and Harry, looking through the glass panels, saw Mr. Mack, the store owner, and two or three other men outside.

"What's the matter? What has happened? Why am I locked out of my own store?" cried Mr. Mack, rattling the knob.

"There's a cheat in here!" cried Harry, unlocking the door. "There he is!" he went on, as Mr. Mack rushed in. "That man tried to pass a bad twenty dollar bill on your boy," went on Harry.

"He did, eh?" cried Mr. Mack. "Well, I'll see about that!"

"You let me go!" exclaimed the strange man. "I haven't done anything. I wanted some butter, but I changed my mind. There isn't anything wrong in that. Give me my twenty dollar bill and I'll go!"

"Oh, no, you'll not—not until you explain," said Mr. Mack, and he caught the man by the arm. Then the man tried to break away.

"Here, help me hold him!" Mr. Mack called to some of his friends who had come in with him. "We'll see what this is all about. Who can explain?" he asked, looking at Bert, Harry and Frank, in turn.

"He can," said Bert, pointing to the former circus boy.

At this the stranger took a good look at Frank, and he seemed much worried.

"I see you know me," said Frank with a smile.

The man muttered something to himself.

In a few words Frank told how he had been cheated by the old twenty dollar Confederate bill the man had passed on him some time ago, in the lumber office.

"And when I saw that man, to-day, for the first time since, hiding around your store," went on Frank to Mr. Mack, "I thought perhaps he was up to some of his old tricks. He went in as soon as you went out, and I saw him give your clerk the same kind of a bad bill he gave me. Only I gave him eighteen good dollars in change."

"But I didn't," said George Smith with a grateful look at Frank. "I was warned in time."

"I tell you it is all a mistake," said the man. "You had better let me go."

"The only place you will go to is prison," cried Mr. Mack. "Take him away, Constable Sprigg," he said to one of the men who had come into the store with him. "Take him away!"

So the man who had cheated Frank, and who had nearly cheated Mr. Mack, was locked up in jail. It was found that he had many Confederate bills with him. That money was once good in the Southern States, during war-times, but now it is of no value, and will not buy even a stick of candy.

Of course grown persons could not be fooled by the Confederate bills, but boys, who had never seen any of that money, might be easily deceived. And it was on boys that the man played his tricks, giving them bad twenty dollar bills for some small purchase, and getting good money in change.

"He just waited until Mr. Mack went out of his store," explained Frank, "and he knew only a boy was left in charge. That's how he tricked me, waiting until Mr. Mason was out of the office."

"Well, you did me a good service," said Mr. Mack, "and if ever you are in need of work, I'll give you a place in my store to help George when I am out."

"I guess Frank is going back in the lumber business," said Bert.

The next day Mr. Mason came in answer to the letter he had received about Frank. He brought with him the bad twenty dollar bill the man had cheated Frank with, and a little later the dishonest man was taken away by a policeman, and put in a place where he would have to work hard as a punishment for cheating honest persons. The Bobbseys never saw him again.

Everyone said Frank was very smart to

catch the cheat as he had done. Mr. Mason received back his twenty dollars, for the man had some good money in his pockets when arrested.

"And now are you ready to come back with me, Frank?" asked Mr. Mason, when everything had come out right.

"I—I guess so," was the rather slow answer.

"My girls are anxious to see you again," the lumber merchant went on. "They have missed you very much. And I want to say I am sorry I was so cross and severe with you," he added. "I was provoked that you should be cheated, but I realize now that it was not your fault. That man made it his business to fool boys with his bad bills. Will you come back, Frank? I promise to treat you better from now on."

"Yes, he will go back," said Uncle Daniel, "but he hasn't had much fun this summer. Suppose you leave him here at Meadow Brook for a while. I think it will do Frank good."

"All right," agreed Mr. Mason. "But my

wife and the girls are anxious to have him home. But let him stay here for a time."

And so happy days began for Frank Kennedy, and the happy days continued for the Bobbsey twins, and their friends and relatives. The long summer days on the farm were filled with good times.

One morning Freddie and Flossie went out in the kitchen where Dinah and Martha were busy making sandwiches and wrapping cakes in waxed paper.

"Are we going to have company?" asked Flossie.

"We's gwine t' hab annuder picnic!" exclaimed Dinah. "A big one!"

"Oh, goodie!" cried Freddie. "And I'm going to take my fire engine to the woods and squirt water on snakes."

"Well, don't pump any fire engine watah on ole Dinah, honey lamb!" begged the fat cook.

"Oh, a picnic! What fun!" cried Nan, when she heard about it.

And such good times as the Bobbseys had when they went to the cool green woods, with well-filled lunch baskets! Mr. Mack, the store keeper, was so grateful to Frank, for having saved the twenty dollars for him, that he sent a large bag of cakes and oranges for the woodland-dinner.

Frank went with the others, and a number of country boys and girls were invited. They played games and sat about in the long grass under shady trees to eat the good things Dinah and Martha had cooked. Freddie played with his fire engine to his heart's content, and, though he managed to get pretty wet himself, no one else suffered much.

And, a few days before Frank was to go back to his guardian Mr. Bobbsey gave the children another treat. They were taken to a nice moving picture show at Rosedale where the circus had been.

After some funny reels had been shown, there was flashed on the screen a schoolhouse, with the children clustering about the teacher.

"Oh, it's us! It's us!" whispered Nan. "Those are our pictures!"

"So they are!" agreed Bert. And they were. Views of the sham battle the children had witnessed were thrown on the screen, and then came a scene showing Freddie. No sooner had he noticed himself in the pictures than he cried out loud:

"Oh, that's me! Now watch me fall in the brook!"

And he did, amid the laughter of the audience.

I wish I had space to tell you of all the other things the Bobbseys did at Meadow Brook, but this book is as full as it will hold. So I will just say that when the time came Frank went back to Mr. Mason's home, and, a little later, the Bobbseys taking Snoop and Snap, went back to Lakeport, there to spend some weeks at home. You may read about the exciting things they did in a story called, "The Bobbsey Twins at Home."

And now, having enjoyed the company of the twins at Meadow Brook, we shall say goodbye to them.

THE END